*Also by Natasha D. Frazier*

<u>Devotionals</u>

*The Life Your Spirit Craves*

*Not Without You*

<u>Fiction</u>

*Love, Lies & Consequences*

# *Note from the Author*

I cannot publish this book without giving thanks to my Heavenly Father, who has been so loving and faithful to me. He has blessed me with the heart to encourage women and the ability to do that through writing. Thank you for entrusting me with such a task. He has also given me a wonderful family who supports my writing career. Eddie, my awesome husband, I love you and appreciate you for all that you do. Thank you for your unwavering support. Eden & Ethan, mommy loves both of you so much. Even though you are still very young, you support me in ways you have yet to understand. Mommy! Thank you for your unconditional love and support from afar. You make sure that everyone knows that your baby is an author. Thank you!  Courtney, Amber, Dad, General Lee, Christine, Vicki & Keisha - thank you for your support.

To my special set of girlfriends who push me to go further and have encouraged me from the very start: Tiera, Toccara & Shenitra - I love you ladies and appreciate your friendship. And to Stephanie - thank you for reading and re-reading.

Readers - You each hold a special place in my heart. Everything I write is to inspire you. Thank you for continuing on this literary journey with me.

Much love & many blessings,

*Natasha*

# Through Thick

# &

# Thin

*(Love, Lies & Consequences Book 2)*

# NATASHA D. FRAZIER

# CHAPTER 1

The theme song to the popular Disney Junior cartoon, Doc McStuffins, had just ended. The first scene playing across the screen was a clip of Doc McStuffins, the toy doctor, having breakfast with her dad. Seeing little children with their fathers, TV or not, always made Raegan both cringe and gush. The scene made Raegan wonder what Carla's relationship with her father would have been like if he were still around. Her daydream was interrupted by the pulling of her hair. It felt as if a few strands had been ripped from her scalp.

"Mommy, where's my daddy?" seven-year-old Carla asked Raegan., after seeing her favorite cartoon character spend time with her dad. Carla stood on the bed behind Raegan combing her hair. They were playing beauty shop, as Carla often liked to do, while watching TV. The numerous trips to the hair salon with her mom had her thinking that she could do everything Raegan's stylist could do, but even better.

"He's gone to work," Raegan played along as she often did during beauty shop time.

"Noooo, Mommy! I'm not pretending. I want to know about my daddy. All of my friends have daddies. Why don't I have one?"

Raegan sighed, picked up the remote and hit the power button. She knew this conversation would come up one day, just not so soon. When Caleb walked out of her life, she dreaded the day she would have to explain to Carla that her daddy was gone. But now was as good a time as any to try to explain something that she didn't really understand herself—Caleb was never coming back. Raegan turned to Carla and screamed, nearly knocking her daughter on the floor when she saw the face of Rico on her child.

Her scream awakened her. It was just a bad dream that surfaced from her guilt of breaking her celibacy vow and sleeping with Rico. Not being able to forgive herself for that was punishment enough, there was no way she could lose Caleb in all of this.

For the third night in a row, Raegan awakened to sweat and tear-stained sheets. The  bad dreams were relentless. They all had the same meaning: Caleb wouldn't stay with her if it turned out that Rico had fathered her baby. Raegan found herself constantly worrying what Caleb really thought about her potentially carrying Rico's baby, and those thoughts even carried over into her dreams. She'd hardly gotten any sleep from tossing and turning. *How will Caleb react if it turns out that Rico is the biological father of my baby?* Raegan wondered.

Before Raegan accepted Caleb's proposal, she'd warned him that there was a chance Rico was the father and he didn't seem bothered by it, but that didn't stop Raegan from being concerned. Would he stay true to his promise that he would stick by her even if the baby wasn't his? Would he change his mind and decide that he wanted nothing to do with her? That her drama was just too much? She felt chills at the thoughts as she gathered the sheets from the bed, along with her silk hair scarf that had come off from the constant tossing and turning, and trudged to the washer as she had done nearly every morning that week.

If she kept up this worrying, she would become sick or kill their relationship. Thoughts had a way of becoming actions. She would no doubt start treating him as if he were going to leave her, making matters worse. She shook her head and wiped another tear that escaped from her eyes as she loaded the washer.

Raegan prayed, "Lord, please help me deal with this in the best way possible." She prepared to shower and dress to meet Caleb. She contemplated whether she would bring up the subject; they hadn't discussed it since she accepted his proposal. She grabbed her purse and keys, set the alarm and shut the door on her way out. The sunlight entered the garage as the door slowly rose. Something about the light hitting her face instantly enhanced her mood, yet her thoughts still lingered around the *what-ifs*.

She popped in one of her favorite CDs by J Moss, and sang along with him in hopes that it would ease some of the anxiety that had been plaguing her for the last few days. She'd said *yes* to Caleb's proposal because she truly believed that he was the one she wanted to grow old with. Their love was strong enough, especially if he could truly get past the fact that her baby may not be his—or so she hoped.

*That was the quickest twenty minute ride ever*, she thought. When she arrived at Caleb's new house, she paused for a moment to gather her thoughts. She had to say something. She needed to ask the question. She needed him to say that he loved her no matter what. Again. Both the steering wheel and gear shift glistened from the perspiration of her hands. She rubbed her hands along her jeans before getting out of the car. *He loves me; I don't have anything to worry about. We can make it through anything,* she encouraged herself.

As she walked along the pathway adorned with perennials and solar lights, Caleb swung open the front door as if he'd been sitting around keeping time. He stood in the doorway waiting to greet her with a bright smile and open arms. He was barefoot, dressed in worn blue jeans and a crisp white T-shirt.

"I love you, Beautiful," his voiced reached her ears as she stepped into his embrace. She needed to hear him say that. Raegan's heart leapt at the confession as if it was her first time hearing it.

"Husband-to-be, how are you this morning?" she greeted him, planting a kiss on his lips and throwing her arms around his neck. She gave him a tight squeeze. His arms around her served as more confirmation of his love for her. Being wrapped in them gave her a sense of comfort and security.

When Raegan pulled away, she grabbed his hand and led him into the kitchen for their talk. She turned to face him, placing her hands on his chest and fired away. She couldn't help it; her nightmares were getting the best of her, so she had to ask.

"Honey, would you take back your proposal if it isn't *our* baby?" Raegan asked, searching Caleb's eyes for conflicting emotion. Since it had been a couple of weeks since he proposed and he hadn't mentioned one word about the baby or the baby's paternity, she needed to know if he still felt the same.

Caleb's eyebrows shot up and then came together in confusion. That was the last question he thought she would ask. He rubbed his hands over his face, slightly frustrated. *What must I do to prove to this woman that she means everything to me?*

"What kind of question is that? Didn't I tell you that I wanted you no matter what?" Caleb understood that not knowing who the baby's father is bothered Raegan to no end. But for him, he was getting what he wanted— her. The baby's paternity didn't matter much to him. He would love the child the same either way. "What do you expect me to say?"

"Don't give me an answer just because you think that's what I want to hear.  I want to know what's in there." She pressed her hand into his chest, covering his heart. She glared at him like a child waiting for her punishment and again she asked, "Would you still want to marry me if it's not a baby that *we* created together?"

"My desire to marry you has never changed, and I think this baby needs loving parents. Will I love the child as my own? Sure. Was I prepared for this? No. Does it freak me out? A little. But it's not enough to make me walk away from you," he admitted. He'd chosen not to dwell on the details of the baby's paternity; he knew that no matter the outcome, it wasn't anything that could be changed and he was prepared to deal with that because he loved her. Pausing for a moment, he asked, "Does Rico know?" He gazed into her eyes, his hands placed on either side of her as she leaned against the kitchen island. Now that the topic was up for discussion, it was best to put all cards on the table.

"No, I haven't spoken with him in a while." Raegan averted her eyes and shrugged, not really wanting to talk about Rico.

"Are you planning to tell him that he may have a baby?" Caleb wondered how Rico would fit into all of this. His problem was more with Rico and how he treated her than her being pregnant.

"No," Raegan slowly replied., "I highly doubt that this baby belongs to him," she said as she tried to convince them both.

"When is the last time you slept with him?" Caleb questioned. He lifted her to sit on the granite-covered island so that they could be at eye level. This wasn't exactly what he had planned for them today, but since she opened the can of worms, they may as well establish the truth.

Raegan wished she was alone outside, reclined on the patio that she could clearly see through the glass French doors that led to the exit. But instead, she was subject to explaining truths that she didn't want to relive at the moment. "It's been a while. Maybe about two to three weeks before you and I got together. But—" she held up her hand, "before you say anything, I had a period before you and I made love."

"I see." He paused, grinding his teeth and staring her in the eyes. She could see his jaw muscles flexing beneath his skin. He never took his eyes away from her, and that made her both nervous and excited at once.

Taking a moment to inhale and relish in the fresh scent of his cologne, she smiled, noticing that he wore her favorite, Curve. It was an old brand but she loved the masculine, sensual scent. Caressing the side of his face, running her fingers along his neatly trimmed beard, she met his gaze and whispered, "Honey, I really would have liked for things to happen differently, but there is nothing that can be done about it now. You will have to take me as I am. And by no means am I going to put any pressure on you. I love you and although my answer hasn't changed, I want you to be certain that this is what you want." Her voice cracked a little, as she glanced down at her belly. It pained her to even think that Caleb would change his mind about marrying her. However, she felt like she needed to brace herself for the worst and give him a chance to be sure. She didn't want her nightmares to come true.

"Did I say I needed to think about it?" He spoke sternly but softly. They were still eye to eye and she could smell his fresh breath, with a hint of peppermint.

"No, you didn't. But I really think you should, babe. I know you weren't expecting me to tell you about a baby when you proposed. Besides, we have plenty of time to make a decision regarding whether or not we want to spend the rest of our lives together. We can continue with the pre-marital counseling, but I want you to be absolutely sure that this is what you want," said Raegan as she placed his hands on her stomach.

"Okay," he said, gently kissing her lips. "But as I think about it, I want you to think about it as well, all right? Remember that I love you, Cami, and I am ready to go all the way with you."

Raegan nodded and smiled, grabbing both of his ears, pulling his head closer so that she could plant a kiss on his forehead.

She loved the way he called her by the shortened version of her middle name. He was the only person who called her that. She smiled inwardly, thinking that he was still taking the news of the baby exceptionally well. She just hoped that she was right and that Rico wasn't the father. She would hate to have to deliver that terrible news.

# CHAPTER 2

Fear crept into the back of Tammy's mind as the realization of Joshua's heart condition set in. Although the doctor told her it was completely manageable, she found herself worrying about him and praying fervently on his behalf. She reminded herself of Philippians 4:6-7: "Be anxious for nothing but in all things by prayer and supplication make your requests known to God."

She sifted through a plethora of websites on her smart phone while sitting in the hospital with him. Based on her research and her talk with the doctor, his cardiomyopathy was manageable and he would likely be okay, but it was still serious enough that it was in his best interest to take an early retirement from the NBA.

A mere cough from him sent her mind racing back to his collapse during his last game a few weeks ago. There he was dribbling the ball to the left and right, leaving his opponents in his trail, only to go up for a jump shot and come crashing to the floor. The thought gave her the shivers.

Tammy had been sitting in Joshua's room waiting for him to wake up. She arrived around 8:30 a.m. dressed in a pair of pink and gray gym shoes with a matching gray track suit. She made it her business to talk with the doctor to get an update on Joshua's condition, because she couldn't handle any more surprises.

Tammy signed in at the visitors' desk, obtained a badge and proceeded directly to the nurses' station. She greeted the nurses on duty before getting straight to business. Before she could finish the question, the doctor appeared at her side. He'd just started making his rounds that morning and Joshua had been his first patient Tammy caught a glimpse of him in her peripheral vision. She had become accustomed to seeing the five foot five inch man with a shiny bald head.

"Mrs. Archer, he is doing just fine today. If everything checks out by this evening, he'll be free to leave in the morning. Texas is where you're headed, right?" the doctor asked as he scribbled something down on his notepad.

"Yes, but not before we are absolutely sure that he's fine. I know you said he would be, but I'd like to prevent any setbacks if possible. I've gone through the literature you gave me and I do believe I understand. I'm just nervous, I guess," Tammy confessed and shrugged her shoulders a little. And that she was—she shifted from one foot to the other as she spoke to the doctor.

"Don't be afraid to call if you have any questions," he reassured her, walking her to Joshua's room.

"Thanks." Tammy welcomed his compassion. She quietly stepped into his room, zipping up her jacket as the wave of air nearly knocked her down. Her sneakers squeaked as she inched toward the bed. She kneeled down to slip out of them so that she wouldn't wake Joshua. She wanted him to have every moment of rest he could get.

"Hey there," Joshua spoke in a groggy voice as he turned over in bed about an hour later and noticed her sitting there.

"Hey sweetheart, how are you feeling?" she asked, sliding her chair closer to him. She quickly stood to plant a kiss on his cheek and then returned to her seat, clasping one of his hands in hers.

"Ummm, better because of that." A smile lit his face after she kissed him.

"I hate to bring this up now, but you do know that I'm not going to let you go back on that court . . . ever." Tammy widened her eyes to stress her point.

"I know." Joshua smiled weakly and repositioned himself to sit up in bed. "In fact, I know that the coach and the association won't allow it either. I really wanted one last season but it's been a good run, though, and now it's time to start looking at other opportunities. I get that."

"*After* you get better. You have plenty of time to worry about that later. I don't want you worrying about that right now."

"Can't wait to get me to Texas, huh?"

"The sooner the better, right? Remember the doctor agreed with me," she said, raising and lowering her eyebrows rhythmically.

"In sickness and in health, right?" he asked laughing. "I'm still your husband and whether or not you'd like to admit it, you're obligated to take care of me."

Tammy thought that he was being rather full of himself, although she agreed with him. And obligated or not, there was no way she wouldn't be a part of his recovery. She'd already felt guilty for not being around to know about his condition in the first place. "I don't mind keeping an eye on you if that's what it's going to take to keep you alive and well." She then proceeded to plant kisses on both cheeks, his chin, nose and then forehead.

"Perhaps I should pass out more often, if this is the kind of treatment I'm going to get from you!" Joshua joked, but Tammy certainly wasn't amused.

Tammy hung her head slightly as she became serious. "You know, babe, I was so afraid when they took you in to surgery. I thought I would never see you again." Tammy's eyes welled with tears at the thought of losing him again and this time for good. There wouldn't have been any going back. No reconciliation.

"Well, I'm here now, so you don't have to worry about that. And since you've agreed to be my wife again, you have me for the rest of my life." Joshua pulled her closer and returned her kisses in the same manner that she'd just given them. Cheeks, nose, chin and forehead. Then he placed a lingering kiss on her lips. He hoped that kiss would somehow signify that he would be there with her until God said that his time was up.

Raising his hand to caress her back, he continued, "Sweetie, with everything that's happened, I don't want to waste any time. I don't want you to ever doubt my love for you. I am no longer that selfish kid anymore, and I'm ready to support you as you pursue your dreams. I'd like to be there for you. Will you let me do that?"

"Yes," she spoke softly, rubbing his hand. She'd been waiting forever to hear him say that.

Interrupting their moment, Joshua's doctor and nurse came in to place an EKG on his chest to monitor his heart for the next twenty-four hours. Tammy watched them carefully as if she thought they might break him.

"Everything is looking great, Mr. Archer," the doctor commented as he flipped through his chart, jotting down notes. "After twenty-four hours of wearing the EKG and we get the results we want, I'll sign your discharge papers and you'll be free to go." He closed the chart.

"So what are you planning to do now that you're retiring from the NBA?" the doctor asked, grabbing his things to move on to his next patient.

Joshua offered more information than the doctor probably wanted to hear—explaining that he and Tammy were reuniting and he was going to take a backseat to allow her to pursue her career goals.

"That's admirable. Get some rest and I'll come by to check on you again this evening," the doctor said before leaving. Patting Joshua's arm with the file, he gave Tammy a wink before exiting the room. He walked back towards the nurses' station and put in the orders to have Joshua's paperwork ready for his release.

"So when are we moving to Texas? Looks like I'll be ready as soon as tomorrow." Joshua grinned. He was looking forward to getting away from the smell of disinfectant and into the care of his wife. Texas had never really been in his plans, but he was ready for whatever it took for him and Tammy to work on becoming one again —no matter what part of the country it took him to.

# CHAPTER 3

"Trash," Raegan said, deleting Rico's e-mail without opening it. Just seeing the message from him made her stomach turn. She didn't know if it was the thought of him or the scent coming from the potpourri sitting on the end table. She realized it was probably a combination of both. She had taken the day off because of the turmoil that seemed to be happening in her uterus. Caleb had stopped by during his lunch break to check on her. As he sat there rubbing her feet, she tried to hide her displeasure at the e-mail from Rico, which was threatening to ruin her day.

*The nerve of that idiot!* She inwardly cursed him. The mere thought of him caused her heart to race and definitely not in the way it had before. She was so angry with him. *Lying bastard. Stay out of my inbox!* She went into the trash folder to delete the message from there as well, as she didn't want any trace of him lurking around if she could help it.

"Oh, no. Not again," Raegan blurted out as she tossed her laptop to the other side of the sofa, slipped her feet out of Caleb's grasp and dashed toward the restroom. She arrived just in time. She hated vomiting and would trade that for any other pregnancy symptom.

Standing at the sink washing her hands and rinsing her mouth out with mouthwash, trying to rid her mouth of the unpleasant smell and taste, Caleb's knock on the door reeled her thoughts back from the unpleasantness. She silently prayed that the obnoxious smell wouldn't capture his senses. *That would surely be enough to make him want to leave. I almost want to.*

Caleb didn't mention the stench as she opened the door for him. "Are you all right? Can I get anything for you, sweetie?"

Raegan tilted her head to one side and smiled. Running her hands over her hair, she shook her head. If there was something that could rid her of the morning sickness, she would ask for that, but what would that be?

He stepped to the side, allowing her to come out of the bathroom. He pulled her into a hug that made her feel as if everything would be all right. His gentle reassuring strokes along her back made her forget about the sickness caused by the baby growing inside of her and the sickness caused by Rico reaching out to her.

"Ouch!" Raegan doubled over in pain, wrapping her arms around her abdomen. She'd never felt that before. Thinking the worst, she immediately grabbed her cell phone to call her doctor with Caleb following closely behind her.

As Raegan waited for an answer, she silently prayed that the pains were not an indication that she was about to lose her baby. Caleb sat next to her on the couch, clutching her free hand in his. He listened intently as she described her concerns through choppy breaths and shaky palms. Within a few minutes of the nurse talking, her body visibly relaxed and he followed suit when the worry began to wash away from her face; her symptoms were normal and everything would be fine, the nurse reassured her.

Caleb didn't realize how much his emotions were entangled at the thought of something happening to the baby.

Raegan was glad that Caleb was with her in this moment. His baritone voice along with his tender touch always had a way of comforting her. She closed her eyes for a brief second to capture this moment in her memory. His cologne. His closeness. His touch and even his breath. She loved him and needed to spend forever with him. She prayed the paternity of the baby wouldn't change any of that for them.

Almost as if Caleb knew what she was thinking, he reaffirmed his position. "Cami, we're doing it together, all the way. I don't do things halfway. I meant what I said, I'm all in." She was glad to have him around to support her. She hadn't even told her mom about the pregnancy; she was so sure that her mom was going to flip out when she relayed the news. She was the golden child. Her brother, as loving as he is, would never let her live this down—getting pregnant before marriage.

The kiss that followed his admission was nothing short of exquisite. For now, she was certain that he would stick around. However, she hadn't told him of her plans to get a DNA test before the baby was born. *Hopefully that won't change a thing.*

Raegan and Caleb were able to recapture the moment they were sharing before her morning sickness and pain nearly sent the day spiraling out of control. Caleb opened the blinds slightly to brighten the room. He used his phone to play soft music, hoping to relax mommy and baby. Then he sat next to her again and resumed rubbing her feet. Raegan picked up her computer to do a little research on DNA testing.

She could hear her best friend Kensi's voice in her ear. *How does Caleb feel about the DNA test? Is he willing to go along with it? Did you even tell him about needing an STD test?* Kensi was often more rational, but Raegan couldn't see past needing answers. She felt like she and Caleb needed to have as much information as possible before the baby came. *There you go questioning his sincerity again,* her conscience reminded her.

"Still checking e-mails?" Caleb inquired. Raegan was rather quiet and nothing filled the air but the sounds of John Legend's voice on the radio.

"No," she articulated slowly, contemplating whether she should tell the truth about what she was really working on. *You said you would be honest,* she reminded herself. "I'm looking up info on getting a DNA test done before the baby is born."

Caleb's eyebrows shot up in confusion. For the life of him, he couldn't understand why she would be doing that, especially right now.

"You're kidding right? Why?" Caleb shook his head, running his hands behind his head. He knew the discomfort she felt about not being certain if he or Rico was the father, but that didn't hurt his feelings any less. All he wanted for her was to be excited along with him that God was allowing her to bring forth life into this world; instead she ruined the moment. His heart was broken.

"You know why." Raegan put the laptop down and slid next to Caleb on the sofa, grabbing his hand. She pleaded, "Babe, I need to do this for me, well for us. We need to know the truth."

"Why does that matter? Especially right now when we're going to be together? Didn't I tell you that it didn't matter who fathered the baby? Didn't I tell you that I would be here for you?"

Raegan nodded. She heard him and at this moment didn't doubt whether or not he would be around, but she needed to know, and deep down inside, she felt like Caleb did too. Maybe not right now but at some point, he'd want to know the truth about the baby's paternity.

Although part of him wanted to know if he had fathered Raegan's baby, he wasn't ready to deal with the reality that there was a fifty percent chance that he didn't, mostly because he didn't want to deal with the fact that she actually slept with Rico. The idea of getting a paternity test made that a reality to him, and that burned him up inside.

Raegan could see the worry in his face from the way his eyebrows were starting to push together. "I'm sorry. I've just been in a weird place with so much of my life out of control; I want to make sure that I can at least have some kind of control with this pregnancy and I think the DNA test will do that for me."

"So what if it is Rico's baby? Then what? Have you decided what you will say to him?" Caleb stood and began pacing. It seemed as if Raegan had already made up her mind about this whole situation without him, and that bothered him too.

"I haven't. I guess we would need to have some sort of a sit down with both him and his *wife*."

"Wife?" Caleb stopped to look at her. "See, I knew something was wrong with that guy!" Caleb murmured an expletive under his breath, shocking Raegan, and slapping a fist into his palm.

"Yea, I'm still trying to figure out the best way to handle that situation as well. I think his wife needs to know." Raegan knew it was a delicate situation and needed to be approached with caution. She didn't want to hurt his wife, but she definitely wanted to hurt Rico, so she had to be careful with that. Seeking vengeance never turned out well. She shook her head at the thought of everything she'd gotten herself entangled in.

"I'm just as upset as you are, but make sure you have a cool head and that you take as much time as you need before you do anything. Please pray about it first. In fact, let's pray about it together. We're getting married, so we're in this together . . . all the way," Caleb emphasized again. Reaching over to grab Raegan's hand, he pulled her into a standing position and prayed:

Heavenly Father, we know that You are all-knowing. We come to You because we know that this situation needs Your touch. We give You praise for who You are and ask that You go before us and make our paths straight. Give us clear heads and pure hearts so that our intentions may reflect Your character. Help us to get out of our own way and handle this situation according to Your Word—in love. Show us how to do that in a way that glorifies You, our Father in Heaven. In Jesus' name, Amen.

# CHAPTER 4

Tammy arranged for Raegan to pick her and Joshua up from Hobby airport when they arrived in Houston. Tammy hoped that riding with a friend as opposed to using an Uber or any other car service would help alleviate any unwanted attention. Rumors were already flying around about his impending retirement before he had the chance to make an official announcement. He was still coming to terms with it himself, so the less people who knew about his current whereabouts the better. He would make his decision known when he was ready.

Cruising her coupe along the curb in the arrival terminal, Raegan quickly placed her car in park and hopped out to greet her friend when she spotted Joshua's tall frame, standing at least another foot and a half higher than Tammy. She threw her arms around Tammy's neck and squeezed as if she hadn't seen her in years. It was good to have another person around who was always in her corner. After releasing her friend, she opened her arms to Joshua as well, hugging him as if he was just as good a friend to her as Tammy.

"It's so good to see you guys. Apologies for the discomfort you're going to feel in this small car." Raegan snickered, gesturing toward her coupe as she moved to assist them with their bags. Joshua immediately swooped the luggage out of Raegan's grip and put the bags in the trunk.

"No problem. I'm sure no one would even believe I could actually fit in there anyway," he commented, brushing off her remark about his size. "And don't even think about lifting anything heavy like that when you have a man around. I'm not that sickly. My hands still work," he reminded the two of them. She shouldn't have been trying to lift anything anyway, since she was with child. As much as the baby had been on her mind lately, she'd forgotten in that second while trying to be helpful.

He didn't have to tell Raegan twice though. She took the hint and walked back to the driver's side and slid behind the wheel. "Hop in guys."

Once Tammy and Josh found a way to fit inside of Raegan's two-door coupe, Raegan shifted the car into gear to exit the airport.

Glancing up in the rearview mirror to get a good look at Josh, Raegan probed, "So Joshua, how long are you here?"

"Indefinitely," he answered with a huge grin on his face. He leaned forward to kiss Tammy, reiterating his joy at being able to spend the extra time with her. No more plane rides keeping them apart.

When he pulled away, Tammy winked and smiled back but added nothing to his response. Raegan asked more questions. "What about ball?" Raegan was prying. She pretty much had her answer to that question but wanted to make conversation. Besides, it wasn't every day that she had a pro basketball player riding in her backseat.

"I'm putting ball aside for now to focus on my health. Gotta stay strong for my sweetheart, you know," he answered, not giving much detail, reaching forward to give Tammy's arm a quick rub.

Since she wasn't getting anywhere with that line of questioning, she shifted her focus to Tammy, who seemed to be lost in her own thoughts.

"So Tammy, what do you have planned for Josh during his stay?" Raegan changed the subject, a huge grin covering her face. She was mostly teasing.

"I haven't gotten that far yet, but I'm sure we can figure something out. He really needs to rest for a while, so we're probably going to lay low and keep things nice and easy," she answered, shifting her body to peer around to the backseat to get a glimpse of Joshua's expression. Joshua looked pretty uncomfortable, buckled in his seatbelt with his legs stretched to the other side of the car. He simply smiled at her. He knew there could be no protest at this point. He wanted to find a court and play basketball, but Tammy would never have that.

"I see. Well, if you guys are pressed for something to do, you can always come over to my place and help me prepare the nursery," Raegan said, glancing over quickly at Tammy to catch her reaction.

"Nursery?" Confusion covered Tammy's face as she reached over and touched Raegan's stomach. "Wait, are you having a baby? When did this happen?"

"Looks that way for now." Raegan shrugged her shoulders and smiled weakly as she patted her belly. She waited for Tammy to absorb the news as silence filled the car for a brief moment. Nothing could be heard but the wind that seeped through the windows as her speed increased around the freeway and the soft R&B music playing on the radio, which seemed to have Joshua's attention.

"Ah! Congratulations!" Tammy squealed in excitement but just as quickly calmed down. She knew Raegan had been practicing celibacy—or so she thought. She didn't want to get into all of that in front of Joshua, so instead she waited on Raegan's reaction. *Is Raegan excited about the baby?*

"Thanks, Tam. You know it's not happening the way I thought it would but it's done now." Raegan caught the confusion in Tammy's eyes, hoping that she'd answered the question that was never asked with the shrug of her shoulders.

"Is Rico the father?" Tammy whispered. She silently hoped that Raegan would say no. It was best if he stayed out of her life forever. Tammy felt a little responsible for Raegan's disastrous relationship with Rico since they did meet at one of her house parties.

Raegan peered up into the rearview mirror to see if Joshua was paying attention or engrossed in the music on the radio. She didn't like addressing that question. She hardly knew Joshua and didn't want him to form a negative opinion of her so early because of the unfortunate situation she'd gotten herself into.

Raegan looked over at Tammy and lifted an eyebrow as she shrugged her shoulders once more.

Tammy mouthed, "Caleb?"

Again, Raegan shrugged her shoulders as if to say, "I don't know." Tammy knew this was a conversation for another day and decided to drop it. She leaned back in her seat floored at what Raegan just admitted. She silently prayed, *Lord, have Your way,* as she didn't know what else to say or pray. She would talk to Raegan about it later, as she was certain that having the conversation in front of Joshua would make her uncomfortable.

"Are you guys going straight to your house, or do you need me to take you somewhere else first?" Raegan changed the subject. If they continued whispering, Joshua was sure to become suspicious.

"Home is just fine," Tammy answered with a wave of her hand. "Thanks for the offer but we want to get settled in. I'll run out later to buy a few groceries."

Pulling up to Tammy's home, Raegan shifted into park and got out of the car. She pressed the button to push her seat forward in an effort to help Joshua untangle himself and exit the cramped car. She popped the trunk so that Joshua could get their bags and went around to the passenger side and embraced her friend.

Tammy whispered in her ear, "We need to talk soon. Take care of yourself."

Raegan nodded before giving Tammy one final squeeze. Tammy broke the embrace, gave Raegan's hand a reassuring tug, linked her hands in Joshua's and led him into the house as quickly as possible to avoid any unwanted attention from her neighbors.

# CHAPTER 5

Raegan's appointment to have the DNA test was in two days and it loomed over her head, especially since she had yet to gather what she needed from Caleb. Because he wasn't on board with having the test done, she planned to test him without his knowledge. He saw no use for such a test since he agreed to raise the baby as his own and marry her. In his mind, she was only further complicating things by getting the DNA test.

She walked around the kitchen island, tapping her chin with her forefinger in deep thought. The best she could come up with was either a soda can or his toothbrush, neither of which he left hanging around. Her thoughts were interrupted by the ringing of her doorbell.

Gliding across the cold floor with bare feet, she flung open the door, embraced Caleb and invited him. Then she ran to put on her ballet slippers and give herself a pep talk to go through with getting what she needed from him, without his agreement.

"Come right on in," she said over her shoulder as she rushed into the bedroom, but not before taking a detour to run into the kitchen, putting the paternity test literature away into the top drawer of the island. She was sure that would change the mood between them in the blink of an eye if Caleb saw it.

Calmly walking out of the master suite back into the living room, she grabbed Caleb's jacket to hang in the closet. "So how has your day been so far?" She tiptoed to kiss him before walking away.

"Not bad. It's been productive. Why are you running around here like a chicken with its head cut off?" Caleb asked as he sat down on the sofa. He was dressed in a crisp white shirt along with a red tie that exuded power and black slacks. Feeling around the cushions for the remote control, he loosened his tie and patted the seat next to him as Raegan walked back into the room.

"Just needed to get my slippers. See?" She flexed her foot around, showing off her footwear. "I didn't realize just how cold the floor is until now." Not to mention, she also needed to hide those documents without looking too suspicious.

"It smells good in here, by the way. What is that? Lemon-pepper chicken?"

"Something like that. You'll see in about thirty minutes." She sat next to him on the sofa and handed him the remote. "I think this is what you're looking for."

Caleb thanked her by leaning over to greet her with another kiss "I missed you, Cami," he said, breaking the kiss, his face only about an inch or two away from hers. Relaxing, he put his arms around her and stared intently, trying to figure out what was up with her. He could sense something was going on, but he couldn't quite put his finger on it.

"And I missed you. I always do." Raegan was still preoccupied with thoughts of the paternity test, when suddenly what seemed like the perfect idea came to her. She would cook broccoli instead of green beans as a side dish, in an attempt to get Caleb to brush his teeth before leaving. Excited about her idea, she hopped off the couch, leaving Caleb to the television, and went into the kitchen to finish cooking. Just in case the toothbrush idea didn't work, her backup plan was the soda can.

After steaming the broccoli in the microwave, their meal was now complete: baked chicken, broccoli, brown rice, and crescent rolls. As Raegan prepared the plates, Caleb eased behind her and planted a kiss on her collarbone. He got a whiff of her perfume. She was wearing a scent called The One; from his perspective, she was definitely that. "May I help you with anything?" he asked and nuzzled his face against her neck once more to revel in her scent.

"Sure, pour me a glass of water and help yourself to a can of soda if you like," she said, peering over her shoulder at him, hoping that he would go for the soda can. Caleb stepped away from her and did as she asked. "Thanks, babe." Raegan set the table, took a seat and waited for him to join her.

Caleb prayed, "Heavenly Father, thank you for allowing me to share time and space with this beautiful woman. Please bless her immeasurably and give her peace beyond her understanding. Thank you for this food and for the cook. In Jesus' name, we pray, Amen." Raegan also said "Amen" in agreement.

After prayer, he opened the soda can and took a sip before taking a bite of food. *Success!* she thought. She wasn't sure if that was enough for the test, but she was definitely going to use that can.

Raegan now sported a huge smile. She was now able to get her test results and she didn't have to *force* the situation. However, she was still planning to get him to use a toothbrush after dinner, as a back-up plan.

Raegan felt like a huge weight had been lifted from her shoulders. She relaxed and enjoyed dinner with Caleb. She almost hated to get the test done because he was so excited about the baby; plans for the baby mostly consumed his conversation during dinner.

"I have a surprise for you," he said after he ate his last bite of food.

"You know I love surprises–good surprises. What is it?" she asked, her eyes glowing, unable to contain her excitement. She put her fork down, not wanting to eat anything else, because all she could think about was this surprise he had for her.

Without saying a word, he got up from the table and went outside to his car. He returned with a huge Babies "R" Us bag. He had purchased a breast pump, diapers and baby toys.

"So where is *my* surprise again?" she joked, arms folded, beaming over the baby gifts.

"Well, I guess they're for the benefit of the little person growing inside of you." He squatted in front of her and rubbed her stomach. "I already know what you're thinking and I don't want to hear it. Forget all of your worries for once and live in the moment, my mommy-to-be. Just enjoy it, okay?" Caleb lavished her with kisses to her cheeks and lips. He was more than thrilled about the baby, not giving an ounce of thought to the fact that he might not be the biological father.

"I will. Thanks," she muttered. Although she loved gifts, she was hoping that he wasn't purchasing them under the pretense that the baby was his. She would not be able to bear the disappointment in his eyes if it weren't so, although she was pretty sure that the baby was his. She just needed to validate her thoughts with the paternity test and then all would be well and she could move on.

"Hey, I need to brush my teeth." Raegan sucked her teeth. She had to keep her plan in motion. "I have an extra toothbrush if you want to brush yours as well."

"Okay, thanks." He thought that was weird but decided to take Raegan up on her offer. How could he turn down an offer to freshen up? It wasn't like he had a toothbrush lying around in his car. He placed the baby items back into the bag and carried them into Raegan's bedroom, following her into the bathroom to brush his teeth.

Without saying a word, she reached under the sink and opened a new multi-package of toothbrushes. "Here you go," she said, handing a toothbrush to him.

When Raegan began brushing her teeth, she had to step out of the bathroom. Standing next to him, watching his unknowing face in the mirror was too much for her. Somehow she felt that he could see right through her and if she stood there any longer, he would figure it all out. But she was so close to putting this all behind her, she had to keep going. She grabbed a small Ziploc bag for his toothbrush from the kitchen. She slid the plastic bag into the front pocket of her linen pants and went back into the bathroom.

Finishing her routine with mouthwash and floss, she replaced her toothbrush and went back into the living room to wait for him.

"Ahh," Caleb said, exhaling a long breath, as he walked toward Raegan to kiss her. "You know I can't resist those beautiful lips now, right?" He leaned over her to plant a kiss on her lips. Immediately Raegan melted in his arms, but that moment was short-lived. She pulled away, not because she wanted to, but she remembered the plastic bag in her pocket. She didn't want him to hear the rustle of the plastic and question her motives.

"Is everything okay?" Caleb looked concerned. It wasn't like her to break away from a kiss so soon.

"Yep, couldn't be better. I'm a little tired though. This baby is wearing me out, so I need to get some rest," she consoled and then emphasized her exhaustion with a stretch and a rub to her stomach.

"You should get some rest. I'll give you a call later," he said, pulling her close and planting a kiss on her cheek before heading for the door. "I'll let myself out. You just relax." He walked her over to the recliner and helped her get comfortable, handing her a blanket and the remote control. With one more heart-melting kiss, he was gone, leaving behind the scent of his cologne.

The second Raegan heard his car door close and engine start, she hopped out of the recliner and ran into the kitchen to fish his soda can out of the trash, placing it into a Ziploc bag, and then headed into the bathroom to put his toothbrush in the Ziploc bag she had crumbled in her pocket. She was so engrossed in what she was doing that she didn't hear Caleb come back into the house to get his jacket.

When she entered the living room, Caleb was standing in the middle of the floor putting his jacket on. Startled, she dropped both Ziploc bags and stifled a scream. "Hey, I didn't mean to scare you, I just left my jacket in the clo—" he began, stopping mid-sentence when he saw the plastic bags hit the floor.

Walking over to her and picking the items off the floor, he held them up in the air. Confusion clouding his face and hurt evident in his eyes, he asked, "Cami, please tell me you're not doing what I think you're doing?"

# CHAPTER 6

After vacuuming her home office like a madwoman, Tammy straightened the books on her six-foot contemporary cherry-oak bookshelf, filled with romance novels, devotionals and business leadership titles. Dressed in sweats with a silk hair scarf tied around her head, she frantically cleaned, dusted and wiped down windows. Her home was about to be presented on national television, and there was no way she would allow it to be anything less than perfect.

Instead of flying back to Boston, Tammy and Joshua decided that it would be best that Joshua make his NBA retirement announcement from Texas. Although far from the size of Joshua's home in Boston, Tammy's home had extra space that the crew could work with in order to make Joshua comfortable and the room presentable for live television.

"Sweetheart, are you sure you want all the cameras in your home like this? We could have easily done this back in Boston where we wouldn't have to put you through all of this trouble, you know?" Joshua reminded her, wiping sweat from her brows.

Tammy nodded and flipped over his palm to kiss it. She reminded him that it was now they're home and less stress on his heart if they kept things simple by having the press conference in Texas, without him needing to travel. She then rearranged the location of her L-shaped desk. "And this is keeping it simple?" he asked, taking both of her hands into his to keep her from moving the heavy furniture.

"Yep," she stated as a matter of fact, slipping both hands out of his grasp and placing them on her hips. It only seemed like a matter of seconds before the doorbell rang with the camera crew. Although the press conference wasn't set to begin for another four hours, the crew had already arrived. Joshua was also going to have a teleconference with his team before going live to announce his early retirement from the NBA.

Joshua left her to the cleaning and went to answer the door and welcome the crew. They walked in ready with their own set of props and screens to make things presentable the way they wanted.

Joshua stepped to the side to allow the team inside the house. They entered the house with cameras, lights, chairs, tripods, and the works. One would think that they were about to shoot a movie and not a five- to ten-minute press conference.

Tammy entered the living room and watched in amazement as the slew of people entered the house with all of their equipment. "Maybe I underestimated this event a little bit?" she asked looking up at Joshua. "Does it really take all of this?" she whispered, standing on her tiptoes to get closer to his ears.

"Of course it does. Do you know who I am?" he joked. "Let's head to your office. We've got work to do."

*These people really are professionals,* Tammy thought. They were already halfway set up, adjusting the lighting and making sure everything would be just right for the next few hours. *Do they really all have to wear black as well?* she thought to herself in observation. *This is interesting.* She figured she would sit in a director's chair or something and watch the conference like any other observer, but Joshua had a different idea.

"You should wear something else for the camera, sweetheart," he leaned over and whispered into her ear as she stood watching the camera crew work their magic.

"What?" She glanced down at her T-shirt and sweatpants. She thought she looked fine for sitting behind the cameras. She did plan to take off the head scarf and slip into a pair of jeans but that was about it.

"Yeah. There is no way you're not going to be by my side in all of this. I want you by my side in every way possible, as you have been the last couple of months, and this is definitely not the time for exceptions. Plus, I could really use your support," he urged, squeezing her hand.

Trying to mask her excitement, Tammy left the room to find something appropriate to wear for national television. She didn't think that she would be on camera but welcomed the opportunity to stand by Joshua. But now she was nervous. She wasn't prepared for this.

As if he knew her thoughts, Joshua stepped out of the room and called out to her, "You don't have to be nervous." She briefly turned and smiled before walking into the bedroom to rummage through her closet.

When Tammy was just out of earshot, his phone rang. It was his coach. News reporters and journalists were already on the scene ready to cover his story. One of them was Kensi, a good friend to Tammy and Raegan's best friend. Her covering his story meant a great deal to her career and she jumped at the opportunity. Her relationship to Tammy would help make her story better than anyone else's since she was able to talk personally with him from time to time. Now, she only needed to ask a few more questions to complete her story.

The coach handed the phone to Kensi and she began asking questions and clarifying facts. She took a couple of minutes to run direct quotes by him before they would be printed. She was one of the best journalists in New York and she planned to make this story one that would open up more opportunities for her, not just in New York, but all over the country. He had been one of the most valuable players within the last ten years and it would be a huge milestone in her career to be able to cover his story. She was pretty sure her promotion was riding on this one piece.

Joshua kept watching the clock. He had never known time to move as fast as it did within the last hour. Nearly three hours had passed since the camera crew arrived, and it was now time for him to start the teleconference with his team. After getting pinned with his microphone and positioning himself as instructed by the camera crew, he slightly bowed his head in silent prayer for strength to get through the rest of the day. As he lifted his head, Tammy walked into the room dressed in an elegant hunter green sheath dress and a pair of black pumps. She had pinned her hair into a bun with a pearl-laced pin sticking out of it. Her necklace and earrings were also adorned with pearls. She moved to his side and helped him adjust his lapel mic and tie before the cameras turned on. She took a seat next to him, gave him a loving smile, took a deep breath and turned to face the world.

Joshua nodded to the director to signal that he was ready. Immediately, they were able to see the basketball team on the screen. A smile spread across his face as he watched his teammates cheer and toss signs in the air that screamed, "Good Luck," "Get Well," "Boston will miss you," and "Stay strong."

"Josh! How are you feeling? How is Texas treating you?" the coach asked.

Shifting slightly in his seat, he answered, "I'm doing well, Coach, feeling much better these days." He glanced over at Tammy and smiled.

"We're all glad to hear that." His tone became more serious as he said, "We want you to take care of yourself and not worry about the game. You had a great career and were truly an asset to our team. Come visit us whenever you're ready. Remember that your health is more important than your career." He paused. "Take a look at this."

Now flashing across the screen were Joshua's career highlights over the length of his career. Tammy was amazed at how much she'd missed and just how great of a player he really was. She glanced away from the screen to look at him. Noticing that his eyes were glistening, she took a handkerchief and dabbed at his eyes and mouthed, "It's okay."

After the screening finished, the coach and team appeared on the screen again. "Those were some great times. That is our tribute to you. Whatever is next for you, I'm certain that you'll do well," the coach said.

Other teammates chimed in with encouraging words when the coach finished. Joshua was touched by the amount of love and support he was receiving from both Tammy and the team. He was now becoming more excited about the next chapter of his life, especially with Tammy by his side. The screen went off and the makeup crew wiped the perspiration from his forehead, touched up Tammy's make-up, and prepped them for the next phase of the airing—the press conference. It was now time for Joshua to make his official statement.

After the director had counted down on his fingers from five to one, they were on live television. Beginning his statement, Joshua said, "I would like to thank everyone who supported my career and my team. This has been an experience that I will hold close to my heart for the rest of my life. It is because of your encouragement and faith in me that I am able to move forward, knowing that I have done my very best and have always played to the best of my ability. Although I have gone through a few medical challenges that are causing me to bring my time on the court to an end, I am thankful that God has given me another opportunity to continue to pursue my passion. It is my hope that each of you will do the same thing: Go after your dreams and pursue your purpose! Replace your fear with faith and make every moment count. Take nothing for granted and be intentional and strategic about everything. God bless each of you!" Joshua placed two fingers to his lips and then covered his heart.

Joshua let out a sigh of relief after his announcement, raised Tammy's hand to his lips, and brushed it with a kiss. Several reporters now gathered in the room with his team and asked questions about his next move. Joshua explained that he had several opportunities but had not yet decided upon one. However, he made it clear that he was off the court but not out of the game.

# CHAPTER 7

"It seems as though you're intent on doing exactly what it is you want to do, regardless of what I think. Is that right, Cami?" Caleb dangled the Ziploc bag in the air. His voice was filled with disappointment and the grin he wore when he left moments ago was long gone.

Raegan could see the pained look in his eyes. She hated that what she needed to do for herself hurt him, but she felt like she had no other choice. Hearing him say her name like that made her decision even harder, but she couldn't let that stop her.

"I thought you understood that I needed to do this . . . for me."

"I, I, I! Seems that the only person you're thinking about here is yourself! It's not just you anymore Cami. Remember that we're building a life together. Is it not enough that I'm going to be here with you through it all?" Caleb was amazed at her selfishness, especially after the moment they recently shared over the baby gifts he purchased. She had just promised that she would live in the moment, but it was clear to him that she took that literally—a moment—and now she was back to playing detective.

Raegan walked over to him, wrapped her arms around his waist and snuggled in close to him. Caleb reluctantly returned the hug, but not as tightly as she would have liked.

The last thing she wanted to do was hurt him, she thought, as she listened to the sound of his heartbeat. As the moments passed, the rhythm escalated and she knew he was upset. There would be no reasoning with him. This would just have to be something they disagreed about. "Having you around is enough, but that isn't the point. Aren't you the least bit curious about this baby's paternity?" Raegan backed out of the embrace, held his waist, and stared up at him. His face was still, his emotions unreadable.

Caleb removed Raegan's arms from his waist and handed the Ziploc bags to her. "Do whatever you think you need to do. If this doesn't work, let me know if you need hair follicles," was all he said. He kissed her forehead and turned to walk out of the door. Sure he was curious, but he didn't think it was necessary to go through such lengths to find out. They were going to be a family and that was enough for him.

∞

Joshua had given Kensi the okay to print her story the same day of his televised press conference. She was glad to have Tammy as a connection. There had to be some truth to the notion that there are only six degrees of separation between any two people.

Satisfied that she was the one to write the story first, she pushed thoughts of work out of her mind to fulfill her duties as accountability partner to Raegan. She vowed to check on her regularly either via phone call or text, whenever Raegan was on her mind. She partially felt responsible for Raegan's sexual slip-ups, because she didn't hold her accountable as she knew she should have.

"Hey you!" Raegan smiled into the phone. "How are you girl?" Raegan asked in a tone that sounded as if she was a native New Yorker.

"I'm well. How are you and that bundle of joy you're carrying?" Kensi asked.

"No issues over here, other than the obvious 'who's the daddy' question," Raegan said, trying to make light of the issue plaguing her thoughts to no end. She reached down to rub her stomach as if to reassure both herself and the baby that all would turn out well for the two of them.

"Raegan, don't stress yourself out over that. Didn't Caleb already say that he's going to stick around whether the baby is biologically his or not?" Kensi reminded her, just as Caleb had continuously done. Kensi curled up on her sofa with her feet under her and muted her television to give Raegan a pep talk. She understood that Raegan was going through somewhat of a stressful time, mostly because things weren't happening the way Raegan would have liked—marriage before baby—so Kensi did her best to encourage her friend.

It wasn't as if Raegan didn't welcome the encouragement, but she felt like Kensi couldn't relate to what she was going through. Kensi wasn't the one who went from being celibate to pregnant and not knowing who the baby's father is. And she surely wasn't the one having nightmares about her fiancé walking out on her.

"I am single, pregnant, in my thirties, and I don't even know who the father of my child is." Without giving Kensi a chance to respond, Raegan blurted out, "But that's all going to change. I am getting a DNA test to find out so that I can have peace of mind throughout the rest of my pregnancy," Raegan said with finality.

Almost as confused and frustrated as Caleb, Kensi attempted to convince Raegan that she was making a mistake. Kensi had not quite been in the same place as Raegan, but she had been in a terrible place. Lonely. Afraid. She miscarried a few years ago, and that was part of the reason she decided to become celibate. No one could help her. No one could bring her baby back. No one could understand. There was no way she could handle that type of pain again. The only person she was able to turn to was God.

Ever since then, that is exactly what she did—find her peace in God. Closing her eyes for a brief moment in an attempt to once again forget the pain, Kensi said, "Raegan, just be ready for what you may find out before you go to that clinic. Have you thought about what you're going to do if the baby is Rico's? Are you even going to tell him?" Raegan was known for leaving out important details.

Kensi sounded like Raegan's conscience, however, Raegan knew what needed to be done. What did Caleb and Kensi expect her to do? Never find out the truth? Wait until her baby was born to find out? She knew that things needed to be handled sooner than later. The earlier she found out, the sooner she could make sure that she would have nothing more to do with Rico's lies and deceit. She could put him, and all of the mistakes she made with him, out of her mind for good.

"I'll work it out, Kensi." Raegan ignored Kensi's plea and got ready to end the conversation.

"Rae, please just hear me out. Am I not your accountability partner?" Kensi questioned.

Raegan let out a frustrated sigh in response. Kensi was right, but Raegan didn't want to listen to her. She had already made up her mind about getting the test done; there was nothing Kensi or Caleb could say that would make her change her mind. She was certain that getting the DNA test was the best thing to do.

"Tell me . . . what does Caleb think about this? He is your fiancé, remember?" When Kensi was greeted with silence she said, "At least tell me that he knows about it and you're not planning to keep this from him too."

"Since I promised to be honest with you . . . I wasn't going to tell him. I just figured I'd get confirmation about the baby's paternity and put it behind me, but he caught me with his toothbrush and a soda can he drank out of."

Kensi slapped her palm against her forehead, shaking her head from side to side. She had no idea what had gotten into her friend over the last few months. She was running out of advice to give, especially since Raegan wasn't taking any of it.

"Caleb loves you; don't hurt him again."

"I know that, Kens, but this isn't about him," Raegan tried to convince Kensi. For the life of her, she couldn't understand why they couldn't see that this was necessary. Regardless of who understood or not, the decision had already been made. She owed it to herself and her baby. The test was as good as done.

# CHAPTER 8

Raegan was one step closer to finding out the truth. Caleb's toothbrush and soda can were stored away in a plastic bag in her purse. She sat in the car in front of the clinic, heart racing and mind swirling with a plethora of thoughts. After the collection technician took a blood sample from her and compared it with the forensic items she brought to test Caleb's DNA, her life could change forever, quite possibly in a way that she didn't want it to. She wasn't sure if she was prepared for that, but she convinced herself that this was the only way.

Her palms became even more clammy as she thought about what would soon happen. She rubbed her sweaty hands up and down either side of the steering wheel as if that was going to give her strength. She could feel her head growing warmer, making the hairs on the back of her head curl up. "Okay, girl, get it together," she said to herself in the sun-visor mirror.

Inhaling and exhaling deeply one last time, she gathered strength, collected her things and got out of the car. She wrapped her trench coat around her body, threw her satchel over her shoulder and walked slowly toward the building. The clinic was located in what seemed to be a vacant strip center. There was not much signage and not a lot of cars in the parking lot, considering it was almost lunch time and she could see a popular chain restaurant on the opposite end of the strip.

As she approached the door, she noticed someone walking out wearing a pair of orange scrubs. "I don't think I've ever seen a pair of orange scrubs before," she mumbled, her mind briefly taken off her issues. The man must have noticed her hesitation and invited her inside.

"Do you have an appointment with us today?" he asked, smiling and extending his hand to her.

"Actually, yes," she answered, accepting his handshake.

"Please come on in and someone will be right with you."

The smell of disinfectant quickly grabbed her attention as she entered the glass door. It wasn't a hospital or doctor's office, but it definitely smelled like one. Raegan proceeded to the reception area to check in. To her relief, there was no one else in the waiting room. She was almost embarrassed to be there because she was a professional who seemed to have every area of her life together, except for this.

Maybe that was why she needed to do this. She had to get her life in order as much as possible; the least she thought she could do was get some clarity as to who her unborn child's father is. Moments after she signed in, the collection technician greeted her from behind the closed doors to escort her to an unoccupied room. "Good morning, I'm Mason Banks," he said, smiling. His smile was warm but did nothing to relax her. Raegan could feel the sweat that was on the back of her head quickly drying in the cold office space. The heat was now replaced with what she referred to as cold bumps.

She said a silent prayer as she followed the technician into the room that was only furnished with a table and two chairs. The table was clear except for the technician's pad and two empty vials that were soon to be filled with her blood.

"Do you have any questions before we get started?" he asked, cleaning his hands with hand sanitizer and then covering them with rubber gloves.

"About how long will it take to get the results?" Raegan asked softly, her voice barely above a whisper. She had already been given that information when she made her appointment, but she hoped she would get a different answer, an answer that would be sooner than seven to nine business days.

"It usually takes about seven days." The technician continued his prep work, pushing up Raegan's sleeve and rubbing alcohol on her arm.

"Will you all call me, send me a letter, or will I have to come back here to get the results?"

"We can do it either way. Just fill out this form and let us know what works best for you," he answered, handing her the forms that were on the table.

"Whichever one is quicker."

"We can call you and e-mail you the results. Just make sure you check that box," he said, pointing to the box as if she couldn't read it herself.

"Thanks." She checked the box indicating that she would like a phone call and e-mail detailing the results. After she filled out the form, Mason took the blood sample and explained again how the process would work. At this point, enough of the baby's DNA would be in her blood to compare to the forensic samples she brought along with her. Once the results were in, she would be notified in the manner she selected. Easy.

Thankful that the process did not take more than thirty minutes, she felt a sigh of relief walking back to her car. As luck would have it, Caleb was now calling. She answered, but decided that she wouldn't tell him she initiated the DNA testing process; she wanted things to stay calm between them. She knew he was probably still upset with her; they hadn't spoken much since he found the toothbrush and can in the plastic bags.

∞

"Raegan, is that you?" Raegan's body stiffened at the sound of the voice behind her in the sandwich shop. It sounded much like Rico's. Because of the slight bulge in her midsection, she wanted him to see her and wonder if the baby belonged to him, but part of her also wanted to run and hide because she didn't know the results of the DNA test yet.

Raegan turned slightly in the line to acknowledge his presence with a stare and a half smile. It took every fiber of her being not to slap him in the face.

"Wait, are you pregnant?" he asked. Confusion clouded his eyes. Raegan had a small frame. Although she was only about ten weeks along, her pregnancy was noticeable to someone who knew what she looked like pre-pregnancy. Still saying nothing, she paid for her sandwich and walked away toward the elevator bank, returning to her office.

Rico didn't go after her. He stood in the sandwich shop where she left him, wondering about the baby—just as Raegan would have liked—thinking to himself, *She can't be pregnant. Raegan would have told me. Even after everything that happened between us, she wouldn't keep something like this from me.*

*If she is pregnant and if the baby is mine, how would I even begin to explain this to my wife? She would never forgive me for this.* Their relationship was already rocky because of his past infidelity.

Finally moving away from the spot where he'd been stuck, he turned and walked back to the dealership. He had only stepped away to grab coffee but he decided to walk through her building. He was hoping to get a glimpse of her because he hadn't seen her in such a long time – after he told her the lie in order to break up with her. He had to find out if that was his baby. That was the one thing he'd been longing for that his wife was not willing to give him, because she was focused on her career. A baby would only slow her down and she wasn't ready for the responsibility of being a mother just yet.

Back inside her office, Raegan sat at her desk, pushed aside binders and folders, and ate her meatball sandwich. Midway through her lunch, her office phone rang and she answered without checking to see who the caller was. Placing the phone to her ear, she heard the sound of Rico's anxious voice, "Is that my baby?"

Taken aback by his question, she just held the phone. She was angry that he called her and a little frustrated with his question. In an accusatory tone, Raegan asked, "Does your wife know that you're calling me about this?"

Rico stammered in his response. He had no idea that Raegan knew about his wife. "Wha-what do you mean, my wa-wife?"

"Please don't call me with any foolishness. You need to be talking to your wife and not me. Secondly, if you don't hear from me about this baby being yours, don't call me. Get it?" Click. She hung up the phone, not giving him a chance to respond.

"Not today. He is not getting to me today. All of that is over; at least for now it is." Closing her eyes and taking a deep breath, she vowed to push thoughts of him out of her mind. Maybe she would be rid of him forever if she had listened to Caleb and Kensi and not had the DNA test done. *But would I be pretending that Rico didn't happen? Would that be lying to my baby?*

She convinced herself that the DNA test was best for everyone involved. *What if Rico is the father and there were issues in his medical history or that of his family?* She'd need to know that. What if her child one day found out that Caleb wasn't his biological father and felt deceived? She convinced herself of all the reasons she needed to know the baby's paternity. She couldn't spend the rest of her life not knowing, and she knew a part of Caleb would always wonder as well. She was certain that the DNA test was the answer to her problems.

# CHAPTER 9

Joshua felt as if a huge weight had been lifted off of him after he announced his retirement from the NBA. He had always planned to retire after about ten to fifteen years of playing, but he never thought that he would have to leave under medical restraints. Having Tammy's support meant the world to him; he didn't know what he would do without her. Although their circumstances weren't perfect, he hoped that this could be the fresh start they needed to rebuild their marriage.

When the lights and camera were shut off, Tammy removed her lapel mic, which had only proved to be decoration, and turned to Joshua. "Are you sure you're going to be all right? Basketball is such a huge part of your life and always has been."

She picked at imaginary lint on his jacket, straightened his collar and helped him remove his lapel mic.

"You must have missed what I just said." He smiled. "Just because I'm off the court, doesn't mean I'm out of the game, sweetheart. My agent is already on top of it. He is working to get me a few interviews with some of the local sports radio and television networks."

"Wow! Good for you *but* you know you have to recover first. Although no physical activity is involved, I need to be assured that you're ready. No rush."

"Thank you for the concern but I am gonna go crazy sitting around here all day. My follow-up appointment is in two weeks. When the doctor gives me the okay, I'm gonna have to get moving."

Tammy agreed. She understood Joshua's need for physical activity and need to work, period. But she was excited to have him in her life again and didn't want to lose him so soon, especially for something that could be controlled.

They continued removing all of the audio equipment while the team shuffled around them taking down the makeshift set. With all of the noise going on around them, Joshua remained seated as he pulled Tammy up from her seat to stand in front of him. As if no one else was in the room, Joshua caressed Tammy's cheek before planting a kiss there.

"Try not to worry about me. Everything will be all right, especially now that I have you here with me." He kissed her again.

That eased her worries a little bit. "So what now?" she asked as the crew removed their final items from the home and prepared to leave.

Joshua rose to thank the crew for everything and walked them to the door. Once everyone was gone, he closed the door behind them and turned to do what he desired to do the moment he saw Tammy again at his basketball game a few months ago. He swept her into his arms and gave her the sweetest, most loving kiss, much more passionate than the pecks he'd planted on her cheeks moments ago. Tammy didn't pull back but instead savored the affection that he was showing her. So much had transpired between the two of them in the last couple of months since losing her grandmother, from his proposal to his heart condition and leaving the NBA. And now here he was, standing right there in her living room. She had no idea her life would change so much in such a short period of time. Although there were some things she could have done without, she was pleased with how things were now going.

"Did that answer your question?" He smiled and pulled her closer to him.

"It surely did." She grinned, her head still spinning from the impression his lips left against hers.

They decided that nothing was in the way of them beginning their new life together, so they sat down to discuss plans for their vow renewal ceremony. They would have an intimate celebration, much like before, with family and friends. They didn't want to waste any time since they were both sure that they wanted only each other and so much time had been wasted because of selfishness and miscommunication on both of their parts.

"Thank you for giving us another chance," he added, running his hand along her back.

"Thank you for not giving up on me. You could have remarried and had anyone you wanted, but you still chose me," she said, scooting back on the couch and curling up against him.

"The same is true for you too. I think we both knew where we needed to be—with one another. Make no mistake; my home is with you, Tammy," he reminded her, lifting her chin to plant another kiss on her lips. The vow renewal ceremony had been a long time coming but this time nothing stood in their way— basketball careers or selfish ways. They were ready to put each other first.

# CHAPTER 10

Raegan stopped to check her post office box on the way home from work. *The day has finally come*, she thought, as she opened the box and saw the letter that would give her the answers she'd been seeking. Apparently there were problems sending her the information via e-mail, so it had to be mailed to her—for privacy reasons. Her hand shook a little from nervousness as she read the words on the envelope, "Personal and Confidential. To the attention of Raegan Sanders."

As anxious as she was, there was no way she could open the letter right there. She needed to be in the comfort of her own home. Grabbing the other pieces of mail out of the box, she shuffled them together in her arms without flipping through them, closed the box and rushed back out to her car as the howling of the wind filled her ears.

She drove as quickly as she could without breaking any traffic violations, at least in her opinion. Any cop looking to give a ticket that day would likely think otherwise. She was out of the car before she could let the garage door down.

She ran into the house, shut the door behind her and said a silent prayer, leaning against the door. She slung the mail on the kitchen countertop and ripped open the important letter she had been waiting for. Pushing her curls away from her face, she read and re-read the results, hoping that she was reading them incorrectly.

In that moment, all she could hear was the sound of her heart and the neighbors' dogs barking as if they were in distress. Her feelings mirrored the anxiety that she heard in the dogs' bark. She dropped the paper to the ground and her own body collapsed to the floor.

She was so sure about what the results would be and that having the test done would confirm what she believed in her heart to be true. This was not supposed to happen. There had to be a mistake. Maybe Caleb's DNA had worn off of the toothbrush and the soda can. Was that possible? Did the test have to be performed within a certain amount of time?

"Okay, just breathe," she said, trying to calm herself. "No matter what, everything is going to be all right." But was it? How could Rico be the father of her child? And although Caleb said that he would be there for her no matter what, would he? Were her nightmares about to become her reality? How was she even going to tell Caleb? What would she say and how would she say it?

Raegan stretched out on the tile floor in the kitchen and allowed her thoughts to run wild. The pain from lying on that hard floor was nothing compared to the pain she was feeling in her heart. "How did I get here? How am I going to deal with this when I don't want to even see Rico's face, let alone deal with him for the rest of my life? How can I deny my child the chance to get to know his father?" She continued to wonder aloud. The thought of pretending that Caleb was the father crossed her mind, but there was no way she would be able to deceive Caleb in that way. She knew the hurt that came along when someone kept secrets— especially ones that could hurt. As the hot water streamed from her eyes, she just lay there.

Unaware of how much time had passed, her pity party was interrupted by the ringing of her doorbell. She wasn't expecting anyone. She was about to ignore it until she heard the sound of Caleb's voice. Her stomach twisted into tiny knots, knowing that she had no choice but to reveal the truth to him that evening. *Why did he have to show up now?* she thought. She didn't even have a chance to rehearse what she would say.

Rolling to her side, she pushed herself off the floor and walked slowly to the door, as if she were facing her doom. It was so quiet, she could hear the sound of the clock ticking. The countdown had begun. Peeking through the peephole as if she didn't know who was there, she reached for the doorknob and opened the door.

"Cami, how are you sweetheart?" He gave her a lingering hug and walked past her to the living room. He took a seat and pulled her onto his lap. "I am sorry for coming over unannounced, but I really needed to apologize for how I acted the last time I was here," he said looking into her eyes, pushing a few dangling curls behind her ears. Work and his issues about the DNA testing had been in their way. Other than pre-marital counseling, they hadn't seen each other since he caught her with the Ziploc bags. He'd been cold and distant. They'd talked on the phone for a few minutes each day but tip-toed around the subject of the baby. Of all days, today was the day he chose to clear the air. He loved her and he refused to allow the DNA issue to be the thorn in his side.

*You may take back this apology after you hear what I have to say,* she thought to herself.

"I know that as a soon-to-be mother it must be hard for you not knowing the truth about the baby. It was selfish of me not to expect or want you to get answers. Please forgive me?" he asked, lifting her hands to his mouth, gently placing a kiss on each one.

"Caleb, I forgive you. I want to apologize for going about it the wrong way. I felt like you wouldn't agree to get tested, so I chose to sneak and do it behind your back by tricking you into using a toothbrush and drinking out of a can so that I could have your DNA."

Caleb acknowledged his displeasure with her tactics by nodding and shifting in his seat. But he still remained silent. He gave her hands a reassuring squeeze.

"I accept your apology, Cami. I think anyone would have done what you did, maybe not the same way, but they would have done what needed to be done."

"I think so, but I still want to apologize for even getting you caught up in all of this. If I hadn't seduced you . . . "

"Seduced me?" He threw his head back slightly and laughed. "Cami, we're both adults. No matter what you did, I still had to make a choice and with those choices, there are consequences. This just happens to be what it is."

Slipping her fingers out of his, she stood and wiped her sweaty palms down the front of her pants. She turned away slightly, taking a few steps back in an attempt to prepare herself to give him the news.

"Well Caleb, there is more. I had the test done and I received the results today." She paused, waiting for his reaction. He shifted his body toward her, with his elbows on his knees. Gazing at her as if to say, "and?" he waited for her to continue, the sound of the second hand on the clock ticking away in his ear. When she didn't say anything, he stood and asked, "So?" Her silence gave the answer away, but he needed to hear her say it.

"Biologically, Rico is the father of this baby," she confirmed, rubbing her belly as the hot tears slid down her cheeks again.

He shut his eyes in disappointment at the news. Although he knew there was a great possibility that the child didn't biologically belong to him, it still didn't hurt any less to find out the truth. In a moment he put aside his feelings and pulled a teary-eyed Raegan into his arms. He knew the news must have devastated her as well, and now they had to decide how they would deal with the facts. He was determined to keep his promise and stay by her side, but the challenge now became Rico. How would he factor into all of this, considering he was the father yet married to another woman?

# CHAPTER 11

Caleb loved Raegan and was committed to staying true to his word—he would be there for her and the baby. Although he never intended to leave her, in the back of his mind, he believed that biologically the baby would be his and that he wouldn't actually have to prove his loyalty to her. After Raegan's confession, he took his seat and sat in silence for what seemed like an eternity. Hundreds of thoughts swirled around in his head. Things were about to get even more complicated. He would need to be with her when she shared the news with Rico.

Caleb leaned forward on the couch, hands rubbing the back of his neck. Lifting his head to look at her, he asked, "So when are you planning to tell Rico the good news? Or does he already know?" Caleb didn't really think that Rico knew about Raegan's pregnancy, but he could never be too sure, seeing as though Raegan had become a pro at keeping secrets and taking matters into her own hands.

"He suspects that I'm with child," Raegan confirmed.

"How is that?" Surprise and confusion covered his face. His eyebrows nearly rose to his hairline. He had no idea that she had been in contact with Rico.

Raegan explained her recent encounter with Rico at the sandwich shop. Her stomach turned at the thought of seeing him again. She hadn't quite thought of how she would tell Rico the entire truth because she wanted to keep it from him. She knew that would hurt Rico and that's exactly what she wanted to do – hurt him like he hurt her. However, she couldn't do that to her baby. She would not keep him out of the baby's life if he decided that he wanted to be a part of it; she just wasn't exactly sure how all of this would work.

As if to distract Caleb, Raegan walked into the kitchen to pour herself a glass of water. Still he remained silent, waiting for her to explain how she planned to address this situation with Rico. It wasn't that he was upset; he was disappointed. He knew that if he spoke, she would be able to hear it in his voice. He didn't want her stressed and concerned with his feelings at the moment. He needed her to stay well so that the baby would be okay. Happy mommy, happy baby.

Putting aside his feelings, he went into the kitchen and wrapped his arms around her. Standing behind her, he rubbed her shoulders and then her stomach. Raegan turned to face him and returned the hug.

"Thank you for this. I can't imagine how you must be feeling," Raegan acknowledged. Although he didn't say anything, the pain and disappointment were evident in his eyes. They seemed dark. He looked as if he was carrying a huge burden.

"Don't mention it," he said, covering her lips with his right index finger. He couldn't explain his feelings if he wanted to and this certainly wasn't the moment for him to try. "Just know that I am here for whatever you need. None of this changes my feelings for you Cami. I love you. I still want to be with you. You get that, right? You are still going to be my wife." He lifted her chin so that their eyes could meet. He understood she was vulnerable and he made every effort to assure her that he wasn't going anywhere. He'd waited far too long to be with her.

Her ears were thirsty for those words. She knew that Caleb was serious about staying around, but she felt guilty for allowing him to. She was still having a difficult time wrapping her head around all of this mess and was certain she needed more time to process it all. Definitely before she said one word to Rico. And his poor wife? Ah!

She rested her head into Caleb's chest as he softly rubbed the back of her neck. They held their embrace until Raegan felt the vibration of his phone in his pants pocket.

"You can take that," she suggested as she stepped away and walked out of the kitchen into the living room. She took a seat in the recliner and positioned it to elevate her feet. From what she could make out from Caleb's end of the conversation, he was being called back into the office. Although she was glad he was there, she also needed some time be alone to think.

"Can I call you later? I have to run back to the office for about an hour or so," Caleb said, putting his phone away in his pocket as he retraced his steps back into the living room. "I can come back if you need me to."

"I think I'm fine. I appreciate you coming to check on me when you did. It's been a rough day."

"No problem," he murmured against her lips, kissed her goodbye, and covered her with a blanket before letting himself out of the house.

About an hour after mulling over her disappointment, she pulled out her cell phone and hesitantly scrolled to the number labeled *never talk to again* and tapped "call" on her touchscreen.

When she heard the call being answered, before the voice on the other line could speak, she blurted out, "We need to talk."

"Who is this?" a woman's voice asked. Raegan pulled the phone away from her ear to make sure she had dialed the correct number. Confirming that she had, she realized that Rico's wife must have answered his phone.

Chloe, Rico's wife, pulled the phone away from her ear to see the caller ID name. *Raymond,* the name Rico used to disguise Raegan's identity in case his wife ever looked through his call log. The voice on the line sounded nothing like a man. Chloe thought back to the nights when she couldn't reach Rico and he said that he'd been sleeping, working extra hours at the dealership or out with his boys. Hearing the woman's voice on the line coupled with the name *Raymond* on the caller ID made her suspicious. She hoped and prayed that Rico hadn't been lying to her again after all that she'd put into their relationship.

Raegan hung up the phone. She wasn't expecting his wife to answer. What was she supposed to say? Her heart fluttered and chills ran over her as her phone began to ring, displaying *never talk to again.*

Rico's wife was calling back. She would look suspicious if she didn't answer, so she picked up the phone. She had nothing to hide. She wasn't the one sleeping next to this woman at night telling her lies.

"The caller ID says Raymond. I'm assuming that isn't your real name. Tell me. Who are you and what is it you wanted with Rico?" Chloe asked, fearing the worst—Rico had been cheating again. The one who promised to always be faithful to her. The one who promised "till death do us part." The one who said he would give his life for her. The one who said he wanted to have children with her and grow old together. But yet again, here she was calling *Raymond* because she wanted to know the truth, which she obviously hadn't been getting from Rico.

Raegan thought for a moment. How should she answer that question? Rico had lied enough to his wife she assumed; there was no way that Raegan could do the same, especially since she asked. *What if it were me,* Raegan thought.

"I'm Raegan…we should probably meet to talk about this, if you want to hear the whole truth," Raegan finally answered. Some part of her thought that it would make the situation better if Chloe could see her face and see how apologetic she was for everything that was happening. To see that she had no intentions of ruining her marriage or her life. To see that she was truly sorry and that she hadn't even known that Rico was married when she was dating him. To see that she hoped that Chloe and her husband could work out whatever issues they had, because she absolutely wanted no parts of Rico and she'd came up with a plan to get him out of her life forever..

"Fine," Chloe said a little reluctantly. Her mouth became dry and beads of perspiration formed on her forehead just thinking of what news this strange woman could be sharing with her and why she needed to speak with her husband. They decided on a time and location and ended the call.

Chloe fought to keep her emotions under control when the call ended. Had Rico been cheating again? Her agitation grew as she fixed her hair, dressed and grabbed her purse to meet Raegan. She couldn't believe that she had become that woman – the one who was getting information from the mistress and not her husband. Rico promised that he wouldn't cheat again and he lied, she surmised. Why else would Raegan call to talk to him and ask to meet with her? Starting her car, she promised herself that no matter what, Rico would be on the receiving end of her wrath. There was no way she was going to live the rest of her life with a cheating husband.

# CHAPTER 12

After hanging up the phone with Chloe, Rico's wife, Raegan sat for several moments trying to figure out the best way to handle this situation. She wasn't expecting Chloe to answer Rico's phone and she didn't really expect her to agree to meeting with her. Why did she even suggest it? What is Caleb going to think?

What would she say to this man's wife?

The one he took vows with—the vows he lied and told Raegan he wanted to take with her. How would she tell Chloe that she was carrying her husband's baby? Was it even her place to tell? Should she call the meeting off? *How would I want to be told if I were ever in this situation?* Raegan wondered but quickly dismissed the thought. She didn't even to want to put herself in Chloe's shoes and imagine Caleb doing something like that to her.

Chloe requested that Raegan meet her as soon as possible. She wanted to quickly get to the bottom of whatever was going on with Raegan and her husband. She and Raegan agreed to meet at a local coffee shop that was about equal distance between the two of them. On the drive to the coffee shop, tons of reasons bounced around in her mind of why Raegan would be calling her husband. The only thing she could settle on was that he had been seeing her. Why else would Raegan need to speak with her in person? *Is she pregnant? Does she have a sexually transmitted disease? Is she intent on breaking up my marriage? Is she willing to fight for her relationship with Rico?* Chloe tried to think of the possibilities as she drove. She wanted to brace herself, if possible, for whatever this woman had to say.

Chloe arrived at the coffee shop dressed in scrubs. She didn't order anything but instead took a seat at a small table near the window. Somehow the chatter from other patrons and the ongoing grinding of the blender kept her from losing her mind as she waited for Raegan to show up. She had no idea what Raegan looked like but had a feeling she would recognize her when she entered the building.

Raegan came into the coffee shop dressed in a lightweight jacket, purple blouse, stonewashed blue jeans and black pumps, with her curls loosely framing her face. She was slightly sweaty, although the weather did not warrant perspiration. Espresso machines and soft chatter filled her ears as she locked eyes with a woman sitting alone near the window. Raegan knew exactly who she was, since she was wearing scrubs and sitting alone. She recalled that Chloe was a nurse because of the accolades she read about her during her internet digging of Rico.

Raegan walked over to her and introduced herself, rubbing her hands against her jacket first before extending a handshake. *Is a handshake even appropriate in a situation like this?* she wondered.

Chloe extended a limp hand and held her gaze. She didn't smile but wore a look of concern. Raegan knew that she owed this woman the truth, even though it probably wasn't her place to tell. Perhaps Chloe needed to hear it from both Raegan and Rico.

"So what is this about?" Chloe asked as soon as Raegan took her seat. Her hands were clasped together and her elbows rested on the table as if that would help brace her for the news she was about to receive.

Raegan swallowed and opened her mouth to speak but couldn't find the words. She knew that the truth would likely tear this woman's world apart. She couldn't be the one to do that. *If it were me, would I want the other woman to tell me? What could she say to make me believe her? Would I believe her even if she sounded convincing?* Raegan's thoughts continued to swirl around in her head until interrupted by Chloe's slightly irritated voice.

"Excuse me? Why do you need to talk to my husband?" Chloe pressed, needing answers. She knew she could have gone straight to Rico with this issue, but since she had the opportunity, curiosity got the best of her, and she took it. She needed to hear it from Raegan first, seeing as though Rico had lied to her before. She would get his side of the story later.

Raegan took a deep breath and spoke quickly as if she thought that Chloe would interrupt her. "I was seeing Rico but I didn't know that he was married." Raegan raised her hands in defense. "I didn't realize that he was married until after we broke up. I'm so sorry and I hope you can find it in your heart to forgive me. Even though I didn't know that he had a wife, I still want to apologize to you. I'm sorry for hurting you because I know that this affects you too." Raegan quickly glanced down at her belly. "I called to tell Rico that I'm pregnant and that it's his baby. I've already had a paternity test so I'm sure. I didn't come here asking for anything because I don't want anything from either of you. In fact, I'm perfectly okay with Rico not being in this baby's life. I'm marrying someone else and the baby will be well taken care of.

Although I don't want him in my life, I did not want to withhold the fact that he has fathered my baby. I guess it was sort of my way of giving him an opportunity to tell you everything himself and ask your forgiveness." Raegan exhaled deeply after getting that off her chest.

"Why should I believe you?" Chloe snarled, surprising herself. She had a gut feeling that Raegan was telling the truth, but she needed it all to be a lie. Why would anyone go through all of this trouble? What would be Raegan's incentive to break up what she thought was a happy home? Chloe thought that she and Rico were finally getting back on track, recovering from his past infidelity.

Raegan expected Chloe not to believe her. If she were in Chloe's shoes, she probably wouldn't believe anything another woman told her about her husband either.

"You don't have to believe me; just talk to your husband." Raegan prepared to grab her things to leave. She had said all that she thought she needed to say. She had already asked God for forgiveness. After apologizing to Chloe, her conscience was clear.

"Wait." Chloe grabbed Raegan's hand. "Let's call Rico to see what he has to say," Chloe said, pulling out her cell phone. She knew that this would have some sort of fall-out, but what better way to clear the air than to have both parties present?

Chloe called him at his office. When he answered, she said, "Hey honey, I'm sitting here with *Raymond*." She squinted at Raegan as she spoke.

"Who-who is that?" Rico stammered.

"You should know. Her number was saved in your cell phone. You left your phone at home today and she called. It seems as if there is a situation that we need to discuss."

Rico whispered some expletive just loud enough for his wife to hear him over the noise in the coffee shop. He thought about denying it but didn't know where he would start. Even if he wanted to, it was too late now. He practically gave himself away murmuring curse words over the phone.

"Is there anything you need to tell me, dear husband?"

# CHAPTER 13

Tammy and Joshua continued with their plans to formally renew their vows, since they were only legally separated. They were excited about reconciling and wanted their friends and family to share in the festivities. Even though they planned to have an intimate gathering, Tammy kept coming up with grand ideas; she wanted the ceremony and reception to be a lot nicer than when they married in college, and Joshua translated that to being more expensive.

She and Joshua disagreed on how elaborate they wanted it to be, and the ceremony planning quickly became an area of tension for the two of them. He didn't want to spend tons of money for a one-day celebration, believing their money could be better spent on something of lasting value regardless of their financial status. But she didn't see it that way. She also didn't think that she was overdoing it, more like Joshua was overreacting. He was the exact opposite of what she thought someone of his status would be like when it came to spending, especially for such an event as this.

"Tammy, I love you and you know that, right?" Joshua said as more of a statement than a question. He shifted his body toward her and waved her planning binder in the air. "But some of this stuff is just plain ridiculous. There is no way we're going to spend one hundred thousand dollars on a reception that is only going to last a couple of hours. Plus, our guest list has tripled from the initial one hundred people we agreed upon. I think we're getting a little carried away," he said in such a way as not to put all of the blame on her.

"C'mon. It's not that big of a deal." She added quietly, "*It's not like we can't afford it.*"

Joshua pointed to the list, highlighting everything that he thought was unnecessary. Ice sculptures. Crystal centerpieces. Jeweled stationery. Doves. Authentic crystal cocktail tables. Ceiling drapery. Oversized aisle arrangements. Expensive bottles of wine for guests to take home as a gift from the couple.

"But it's the start of our new life together," she said with a pout and folded her arms across her chest.

"And is this how you want to start it? By frivolously spending tons of money? I'm sorry, Tammy, but this isn't going to work. I think we should stick with our original plans." Joshua tossed the binder on the coffee table and pulled Tammy close, slipping his hands underneath hers so that their hands rested in his lap.

They had yet to discuss how they would handle their financial affairs, and from the looks of things, Joshua knew that he would need to be in charge in that area. He was starting to worry that Tammy had become superficial. He didn't want to deny her the joy of having this experience become a dream come true, but he was sure there was a more reasonable way to do it.

Money would definitely be an issue that they would have to work through. He knew it would be difficult to convince Tammy that it would be best for him to handle their finances—after all, he did earn a degree in accounting before going off to the NBA, so he felt like he was more qualified to do the job.

Joshua knew that spending the extra money wouldn't damage their finances, but he didn't want it to be the start of something more serious down the line in their marriage. If he gave in now, what would it be next? A more expensive wedding ring? Would she demand a certain number of carats? Would it be a vacation home in another country? Or expensive cars? He didn't live his life that way, and the thought of being paired with someone who wanted to live a flashy lifestyle nearly gave him a heart attack.

"Why is it such a big deal? It's our celebration of our new life together! It's one day! Can't you just give me that?" Tammy slipped her hands out of his; she really didn't see why Joshua was making such an issue out of it. They would renew their vows, have children, and move on with their lives. She wasn't planning on spending all of his money; she just wanted to have a nice, intimate gathering with a couple of expensive items here and there.

"You're exactly right! It's one day and we shouldn't spend that kind of money on one day," Joshua said, gesturing toward the binder that outlined the expensive plans.

"You've got to be kidding me! I can't believe we're arguing over this." Tammy stood, folding her arms. *He is being impossible*, she thought. Why should she have to give up what she wanted simply because he thought they were spending too much money?

In fact, she could spend her own money. She earned it. He had no right to tell her what she could do with her hard-earned money. If he thought that he would be keeping an eye on what she did with her money, then he had another thing coming. She was in charge of her dollars.

"Tammy, please sit down," Joshua said calmly. He straightened the binder on the table and sat back on the couch staring up at her. He refused to get pulled in to her emotions. She was being irrational. There was no way they were going to spend thousands and thousands of dollars on one day. There had to be some type of compromise.

With her hands on her hips, Tammy paced several times in front of him, silent. She was fuming at the thought of Joshua trying to take charge of their financial affairs. She felt as if he was trying to run some macho game on her. *I'm the man and you have to do what I say.* She was not going for that. It was her vow renewal, too, and she was determined to get what she wanted, even if he had to be surprised on the day of the ceremony.

Tammy sat down in his lap. "I'm sorry. You may be a teensy bit right," she agreed, pressing her thumb and pointer finger together. "I will downsize it a little so that I won't blow the budget," she conceded, although she had no intentions of cutting as much as she led him to believe.

# CHAPTER 14

After Chloe's call, Rico left a customer sitting in his office, yelling to his coworker to take over for him. That was one commission that he would have to forfeit. He fumbled with his keys on the way to his car, dropping them several times. All of a sudden, his tie felt like it was too tight. He had known that his indiscretions would likely catch up with him, but not in this way. There was no telling what Raegan had said to Chloe, and he knew that lying would make the situation worse with his wife. He never intended to hurt Raegan or allow things to go too far; he had feelings for her but he knew that they could never be. *Is this payback?* he wondered. He never wanted to hurt Chloe either, seeing as though she is the one he took vows with.

As Rico raced to the coffee shop, he tried to come up with the right apology that would appease Chloe and save their marriage. If Raegan had shared everything, which he had no doubt that she did, then Chloe must be dying inside. He banged his fist against the steering wheel in frustration. There was likely nothing that he could say to charm himself out of this; this would be the one time that his smooth talk would not be able to save him.

When he arrived, he parked next to Chloe and hopped out of his car. He ran into the building wearing the look of a deer caught in headlights. He paused in the doorway to see both women turned to face him. Were they ganging up on him? He commenced a slow stride to the table and took a seat next to his wife, looking from her to Raegan, trying to read their expressions.

Raegan did not speak. In fact, she turned her attention toward his wife, hardly acknowledging his presence.

"Rico, choose your words carefully because I'm only going to ask you this once," his wife stated calmly, eyes burning a hole through his skull. "Do you know this woman?" She tilted her head toward Raegan, never taking her eyes off him.

Running his tongue along the back of his teeth, he indeed thought carefully before answering. There was no easy way to tell the truth. Quickly darting his eyes to Raegan and then back to

Chloe, he scooted his chair closer to hers.  "Yes, but please let me explain."

Ignoring his plea, Chloe asked, "Were you having an affair with her?" Her voice became slightly elevated but not enough to alert the other patrons.

"It didn't mean anything. Chloe, baby, listen . . ." he began, but again she cut him off. Meanwhile, Raegan's blood was beginning to boil. *It didn't mean anything?* She could have pulled out the printouts of the countless letters that he'd written to her about missing her, loving her, her being all that he wanted in a woman and him wanting to marry her. But proving her point would further hurt his wife and she wasn't there to do that.

Resisting the urge to reach over and strangle him, she interrupted, "Excuse me, can I say something?" Raegan treaded lightly. She no longer wanted to be in the middle of whatever their issues were. She wanted out, and that was her primary reason for contacting Rico one last time.

Both Rico and Chloe stared at her, Chloe wondering how this woman became a third party in their marriage.

"I don't want anything from either of you," stated Raegan, holding her palms up in surrender. "In fact, I plan to raise this baby without support from you. My only request is that Rico sign over his parental rights to this baby," Raegan said, pulling out a piece of paper and handing a pen to Rico.

She was serious when she said that she no longer wanted Rico to be a part of her life in any way. Even though she was carrying his baby, she had no intentions of raising this baby as his and she wanted to make sure that decision didn't come back to haunt her later. Her baby would be raised as one belonging to both her and Caleb. As far as she was concerned, Caleb was her baby's father, biological or not.

Chloe was partially relieved, but a part of her hurt for her husband. She knew he wanted to have children one day and that was the one thing that she was not ready to give him.

Rico sat quietly. No emotion exuded from him. He was still stunned that Raegan was actually carrying *his* baby—a child that he would never get to kiss, cuddle or love if he signed over his parental rights. This could be his one chance to have the child he always wanted—from his own bloodline. He could give up his opportunity to be a father, or he could put his marriage in further jeopardy and fight Raegan for custody or at least for visitation rights. He and Chloe had talked about getting pregnant but had never moved forward with planning for a child, but now the opportunity to have his own flesh and blood was right in front of him and simultaneously being snatched away.

Rico cared for Raegan but he wanted his marriage with Chloe to work. He'd mistreated her and done things that didn't uphold his marital vows, but he wanted to do right by her even if that meant giving up his chance of having his own child.

Rico took one look at Chloe, accepted the pen from Raegan, and signed his name on the signature line without even reading the document. He thought that would make Chloe happy and at least prove to her that he wanted to put everything that happened with Raegan behind him. Exhaling one deep sigh, he handed the pen and paper back to Raegan, returning his gaze to Chloe.

Raegan's business was complete. She didn't have another word to say to either of them. They were no longer a part of her life as far as she was concerned. She had told the wife all of the information that she would give; anything else Chloe wanted to know, she would have to get from her husband. Raegan didn't care; she just wanted out.

Back in the car, Raegan called Caleb to discuss her impromptu meeting with the couple. She knew he wouldn't be pleased about not being in attendance, but it wasn't as if she planned to be sitting there with the two of them; it just happened. She felt a rush of relief because Rico didn't put up a fight about signing over his parental rights. As far as she was concerned, she and Caleb could now live in peace and leave Rico, and all of the drama that came along with him, in the past.

Raegan drove out of the parking lot and stopped in the left turn lane at a red light. While waiting for Caleb to answer her call, her phone fell to the floor near her right foot. As she reached down to pick up her phone, she heard a car horn. Without paying much attention, she assumed that the car horn was signaling her that she missed the traffic light turning green. Startled, she placed her foot on the gas pedal. Almost immediately Raegan slammed her foot on the brakes, but not before she collided head-on with a four wheeler.

"Hello? Hello? Cami?" Caleb's frantic voice echoed into the phone as he heard Raegan scream and the screeching sound of clashing metal. "Are you there?"

# CHAPTER 15

Raegan drifted in and out of consciousness as the voices around her kept asking, "Are you all right?" Confusion and fear clouded her mind as she tried to figure out where she was and what was going on. The driver in the vehicle behind her called 911 and rushed to her side to see if she was okay.

"Ma'am, ma'am, can you hear me? Are you okay? Is there anyone that I can call?" the young man asked, leaning over against her shattered window. He was careful not to step into any of the broken glass surrounding her car as he made his way to her. Raegan did not utter a word. Her head rested on the seat as her eyes opened and closed.

The young man spoke slowly and calmly in a reassuring tone, "Everything is going to be all right. I have called for help." He wanted to help in some way before the emergency crew arrived but was afraid to touch her. He'd watched enough medical TV dramas to learn that he could possibly put her in a much worse condition if he moved her.

Raegan's body hurt so badly that she was afraid to move, afraid to speak. Seeing the air bag deployed nearly sent her over the edge. Her mind raced to thoughts of her baby and Caleb. *Caleb! I was calling him,* she remembered. She parted her lips and whispered Caleb's name in hopes that the young man could hear her voice. She was right; it did hurt to even speak.

Relieved that she was at least responding, the young man squatted near her window once more in an attempt to hear her strained voice.

"Caleb." Raegan whispered his name again.

"Is that who you want to call? Caleb?" he spoke slowly in a loud voice as if she was the one having trouble hearing.

She blinked in response, praying that he would understand that she meant yes. Hot tears streamed down her face when she thought of Caleb and what may have happened to her baby. Her head hurt more at the thought of it, so she tried her best to relax.

The sound of an ambulance and other emergency vehicles compounded the pain and anxiety.

"I promise to find him for you ma'am. Do you have your cell phone?" the young man asked. Again, Raegan blinked and slightly nodded. The young man thought that it probably wasn't helping asking her questions right now, and he would just search her car for her phone once they took her from her vehicle. He stepped out of the way when the emergency crew arrived.

The EMTs worked to remove Raegan from her totaled car while the police officer questioned the other driver about what happened. The driver explained how Raegan pulled out into traffic and he'd done all he could not to collide with her but it all happened so quickly. He walked away from the crash with a few bruises and a dent in the driver side of his truck; but clearly the woman didn't fare so well.

The witness who had been trying to help Raegan shared his version of the accident and asked the officer if he could look for Raegan's phone once she was safely removed from the car. He said, "She wants to contact someone named Caleb. I promised that I would help find him, but I need her cell phone. If it's all right with you, Officer, I'd like to look for her cell phone to contact him for her."

The police officer extended a handshake and thanked the young man for his time. The officer turned around to see that Raegan was being placed on a gurney and agreed to allow the young man to try to find her phone as he stood close by scribbling notes on his pad.

The young man raced to Raegan's car. He searched through it, trying not to cut his hands on broken glass. He found the phone on the floor near the gas pedal and began looking for Caleb's number. He didn't have to search for very long because her phone began ringing and vibrating in his hands. Caleb was calling.

"Hello," the young man answered.

"What's going on? Where is Cami?" Caleb asked, fearing the worst. He had heard the screeching sound and Raegan's scream. He prayed that she wasn't hurt.

"My name is David and the woman asked that I contact you. She was just involved in an accident and is about to be transported to the hospital." Raegan's car was totaled and she appeared to be in bad shape, hardly able to move or talk, but he didn't want to alarm Caleb.

"How is she? Where are they taking her?" Caleb blurted out while racing to his car to meet her at the hospital.

The young man did not have the answers Caleb was seeking. Instead he walked over to the police officer and handed him the phone. The police couldn't provide any specific information on Raegan's condition, only that they were taking her to the nearest hospital—St. Luke's.

Caleb hung up the telephone and raced to St. Luke's as quickly as he could so that he could see his love. He could not lose her, not when they were finally going to have the life they'd always wanted with each other, not ever. He couldn't stop thinking about how afraid she must be and her concern for the baby. He knew that had been an area of anxiety for her lately, especially knowing that Rico was the biological father. He promised that he'd do everything he could to make sure that both she and the baby were taken care of. He didn't want her worrying about anything. He just wanted her to feel loved and safe.

His thoughts continued to swirl as he pulled up to the hospital. *What would I do without her?* He had to stop himself from thinking and fearing the worst. He hadn't even laid eyes on her yet. Whatever the case was, he had to remain positive. Caleb jumped out of his car, running inside to see if there was any news regarding Raegan.

Amidst his conversation with the nurses at check-in, the EMTs burst through the emergency entrance doors. Caleb spun around to get a look at the body on the gurney—Raegan. Caleb ran alongside the moving gurney, shouting, "Cami, baby, I'm here! I'm here!"

"Sir, you're gonna have to step back," one of the EMTs said, pulling his arm to keep him from going any further, as the other two EMTs pushed Raegan's gurney behind the emergency doors to receive care.

Caleb snatched his arm away, running both hands behind his neck. He felt helpless. He knew that he wasn't supposed to go behind those doors, but that didn't stop him from trying. He needed her to know that he was there and everything was going to be okay. At least he needed to convince himself, because seeing the blood staining the sheet surrounding the lower half of her body didn't convince him at all.

∞

"Is this how you treat me, Rico?" Chloe fumed as her nostrils flared. If it were possible, steam would have been blowing through her ears and nostrils.

"Please Chloe, just let me explain," Rico continuously pleaded, reaching for her elbow. He requested the opportunity to present his case, although he had no idea what he could say to make the situation better. There really was no explaining his actions. He was an adulterer and that was all there was to it.

"Explain what?" Chloe screamed, snatching her arm away, causing the few people who were sitting in the coffee shop to stop and stare at them. Lowering her voice to hide the embarrassment that she already felt, she quipped, "What could you possibly say that would make this any better? It was a mistake? You promise not to do it again? It's over? You gave up your rights to your baby for us? How about not fathering a baby with another woman when you're already married? Huh? You're so ridiculous!" Chloe couldn't stand the sight of him. She grabbed her wristlet and keys, dropped his cell phone in his lap, and walked toward the door as quickly as she could without running.

Rico jumped up from the table and followed closely behind her. He was afraid of what was going to happen next. He had never seen the fire in her eyes that he was witnessing in that moment, and he never wanted to see it again. He had never meant to hurt her; things just got out of control.

"Sweetie, please tell me what I can do to make this right?" he called behind her as she raced to her car to make her shift at the hospital.

Chloe spun around and laughed sarcastically. Tears formed in her eyes and her voice was bitter and cold. "Ha! You can start by packing your things and finding another place to lay your head. I don't want to see any trace of your lying, cheating behind when I make it home from my shift in two days! Get it?" She took a few steps toward him and pressed her index finger into his chest. "In case you don't, let me make it plain for you . . . you ended our marriage the moment you decided that you needed to spend time with someone else," Chloe hissed. She walked away fuming as she slid into her car and slammed the door, not giving Rico an opportunity to respond. As far as she was concerned, there was nothing else to talk about.

"Ugh!" Rico screamed, kicking his car door in frustration. He had no idea that things would go this far. He was so sure that he was doing the best thing for his marriage when he broke things off with Raegan. Now it seemed as if he had no marriage to save; he had already ruined it.

# CHAPTER 16

Tammy took the reins on the planning for the vow renewal ceremony and made several key decisions with little to no input from Joshua. She knew what his response would be to some of the extravagant things she was planning for the reception, so she either downplayed them or neglected to mention them at all.

Even though she'd always wanted to have a nicer ceremony to make up for the simple wedding they had many years ago, she couldn't believe how much her version of "nice" cost. However, she perceived it as a once-in-a-lifetime opportunity and they could afford it, so she really didn't think it should be an issue. She couldn't understand why he was so bent out of shape about costs.

Tammy didn't want something as silly as the ceremony and reception details to get in the way of their relationship. Both of them had far too many friends and acquaintances that didn't even make it to the one year mark of marriage. She didn't want that to be them again. Besides, it wasn't as if she was selecting all the most expensive items; she often went with the less expensive version. The costs were still adding up and she hoped that Joshua would give in just this once and allow her to have the wedding she always wanted. *I will count the costs and better manage finances in a way that pleases him after the vow renewal*, she told herself. That would be her compromise.

"Sweetheart," Joshua called to her from the kitchen. She had been sitting in bed searching the internet for bakeries so they could schedule appointments for a cake tasting.

"Do you need help with something?" she asked, walking into the kitchen. She'd heard the rattling of pans and plates and figured he must have been searching for something. Instead, she walked into the kitchen to find a place setting for two. He had prepared grilled chicken paninis.

He gestured toward the table for her to have a seat. "Consider this my peace offering," he said and smiled. He walked over to help her into her seat.

"Peace offering? Were we at war?" She glanced up at him with raised eyebrows as she took her seat.

"Yeah, something like that. I know we've been disagreeing a lot lately when it comes to renewal ceremony details, so I think we should talk about it." He would be fine skipping the ceremony altogether, but he knew that Tammy desired much more and he wanted to give her that as long as it was within reason. He definitely didn't want finances to be an area of strain in their relationship and felt like it was very important that they talk openly about what their expectations were now that things were much different than they were when they were two college students.

"Okay." Tammy hesitated. She extended her hand to him and waited for him to speak first since he brought it up.

Joshua paused to pray for their food. Afterward, he explained that he wanted her to have the wedding of her dreams but he didn't want her to be misguided about what was more important—their relationship, not the ceremony.

"Sweetheart, I don't want you to think that I'm trying to control you when it comes to money, but I do want to make it clear where I stand on the issue. Even though we're in a pretty solid financial position, we still need to make good choices, even when it comes to this ceremony. I would never deny you the opportunity to have the ceremony you've always dreamed about, because I love you, but we just need to be reasonable."

Tammy chewed a piece of her sandwich as she thought about what he was saying. To her, although he said he wasn't trying to control her, it surely felt like it. If he didn't want to control her, he would let her plan the festivities the way she wanted, although she was doing that anyway. He just didn't know it.

"And that's just it. You're saying that you don't want to control me, but that is exactly what you're doing. It's almost as if you're holding it over my head. We both know that you have millions of dollars. It's like you think I want to spend it all. Remember that I loved you before you went to the NBA; I am not interested in you because of your money," Tammy said defensively.

"Hold on. Calm down. Let's take a step back. I never said that you were interested in me because of my money."

"You didn't have to. But that is exactly what you meant."

Joshua was getting frustrated again. It was just like Tammy to hear what she wanted to hear and flip things around. He knew very well that she wasn't interested in him for monetary reasons. But what he wanted her to see is that he'd managed his finances well over the past several years and he wasn't about to change that and give in to her extravagant wants just because she was ready to wear his last name again.

"Tammy, listen to me," he called to her, leaning back in his chair. "I love you. The only thing I want you to see here is that I want us to manage our finances well, and I'll be in charge of that. I just need you to be on board with me and allow me to do my job. As the head of this family, it is my duty to make sure that we're always taken care of. You must understand that I can't do that effectively if we can't agree on how our money should be spent."

Tammy's eyes widened the moment he stated that he'd be in charge of their finances. She was certain that he meant only his income. There was no way she was going to allow him to manage what she earned. She knew that he would think that implied that she didn't trust him. That wasn't true. It's just that she'd always managed her own money, just as he had managed his, and she'd done well also. She managed to buy a house. She paid her bills on time. She even had a little savings and could purchase a few of the things she wanted.

"What do you mean you'll be in charge?" she questioned. She couldn't figure out any other way to ask without him getting offended. Did he expect them to get joint accounts? Was she to get her paycheck deposited into this account? Was that even necessary considering the amount of money he earned?

"It means that I will take care of our household bills and necessities, including food. For major purchases, we will have to discuss them first, but ultimately, the decision of when and whether or not we'll make the purchase is up to me. Now don't get me wrong, we will both agree to a budget, I'll just be making sure that we stick to it. Think of me as the treasurer," he stated as if that was the end of the discussion, leaning back in his chair with his arms folded across his chest. His demeanor spoke volumes; that was the way it was going to be and no challenge she could come up with would change his mind.

Tammy had to admit that he made sense, but she still wasn't quite comfortable with the idea just yet. Every partnership needed someone to manage the finances. She knew that most businesses and relationships worked well when the parties involved employed their strengths. She knew that he was good with money. When they first met and they both had very little, he managed what little he had. He saved to take her on dates and buy her things for special occasions.

However, she had a hard time relinquishing control. It would take time for her to get used to the idea, but she agreed to work on it. But that was for some future day. Right now, the issue at hand was the celebration of their vow renewal. In her mind, that was something different. She wanted to have her day; she believed she deserved that much.

"You're right and I totally understand everything you're saying. I agree with you." Pausing, she challenged, "So treasurer . . . what are your thoughts about this ceremony we're planning?"

"Start with showing me what you've planned so far." He smiled. He knew that Tammy was probably going overboard. He wanted her to be happy, but he needed to be sure that she understood that this was only one day. He was willing to make a few concessions but not many.

Tammy excused herself from the table and returned with a planning binder. She'd already done most of the work in hopes that it would be too late for Joshua to make her scale things down.

After seeing her selections, he was actually quite impressed. She didn't choose the most expensive items, but she teetered along a fine line.

"All of this is nice, sweetheart; you're doing a great job. And your dress–you can buy whatever dress you want. Consider it an early gift from me."

The smile that illuminated her face warmed his heart. He hoped that giving her a blank check for her dress would cause her to be more conscious of her spending on everything that was left.

"Thank you, honey!" she squealed. She was so excited to have his blessing and not have to be so concerned with whether or not he'd think she was spending too much money. However, she somehow felt like a child in that moment and she didn't like that. They would have to discuss it later, because she couldn't be put in a position where she would have to *ask* to spend her own money.

# CHAPTER 17

Although Tammy had reservations about the whole money issue she and Joshua were dealing with, she felt a rush of excitement knowing that she could buy whatever dress she wanted and there would be no talk of her *going over budget*. She had to pull someone else in on the excitement and the dress shopping frenzy she was about to embark upon. The only person she knew who would very well share in her excitement was Raegan, because she was getting married soon.

Tammy called Raegan to ask her to accompany her on dress fittings, but she kept receiving her voicemail. That was unlike Raegan, so she reached out to Kensi and Michelle to see if they'd heard from her. Learning that no one had spoken to her, she became worried.

She called Caleb. She had his number in case of an emergency, and not being able to reach Raegan right now was an emergency in Tammy's mind.

Tammy called Caleb several times and didn't receive an answer there either. Voicemail. After about four unsuccessful attempts to reach him, he returned her call.

"Caleb, I was beginning to worry. Where is Raegan? I haven't heard from her. Is she with you?" Tammy fired away.

"Raegan was involved in an accident, Tammy. I'm here at the hospital waiting to see her." His voice sounded weak with worry.

Tammy immediately thought about the baby and how both Raegan and Caleb must be feeling right now. "What's going on now? Is she in surgery or something? How long ago did this happen?"

"I've been here four hours. I haven't heard anything yet, but I do believe she's going to be just fine," Caleb said, remembering the blood that stained the sheet wrapped around the lower half of Raegan's body.

"I'm on my way." Tammy pushed thoughts of dress fittings away from her mind and refocused on Raegan. She had to go see her. After getting the hospital information from Caleb, Tammy immediately grabbed her purse and keys, gave Joshua a quick update, and jumped in her car to meet Caleb at the hospital.

"Lord, please let Raegan be all right. I know that You have not given us the spirit of fear but instead You've given us power, love and a sound mind. But right now, I am afraid. I don't know what to expect, so I'm afraid my friend may be seriously injured. She was also carrying her first child. I ask now that You strengthen her right where she is and give her the courage to deal with whatever the results of the accident may be. I know that You have all power in Your hands, so in this moment, I ask that Your power strengthens and empowers us all so that we can be helpful to Raegan in whatever way she needs. In Jesus' name, Amen," Tammy prayed as she drove to the hospital. She did not have a good feeling about this. Being that Raegan was pregnant, that made her nervous. Nervous for both Raegan and the baby. She was far from being a physician, but she knew that trauma was not good for Raegan's pregnancy.

When Tammy arrived at St. Luke's, she threw her car into park and rushed into the waiting area to find Caleb, who sat with his head bowed, face in palms, praying. She didn't say anything when she spotted him. She walked over and sat next to him, placing her hand gently on his shoulder. He glanced up at her, eyes wet, with worry apparent on his face.

"Any news yet?" Tammy asked. She could empathize with him. She understood how it felt to be sitting in a hospital waiting for news about the condition of a loved one. In the past few months, she had to go through similar situations with both her grandmother and Joshua.

Caleb shook his head. "I'm still waiting. I was here when they brought her in, but I haven't heard a word yet. Let me check again," his voice cracked. He slipped his sweaty palms into his pockets and walked over to the nurses' station for the eighth time in the past hour.

"Excuse me ma'am," Caleb said as politely as he could muster. He was ready to start running down the halls, opening up doors until he found her or someone who would talk to him. "I'm still waiting to hear about Camille, I mean Raegan Camille Sanders' condition. She was brought in a few hours ago by ambulance. I'm her fiancé and I'd like to know how she's doing. I don't want to be a nuisance, but if you could please ask someone to come talk to me, that would really be helpful." Caleb spoke as calmly as he could considering the circumstances, but inside he was screaming.

He had been there for several hours and there was not a word. That bothered him more than anything. He knew she was fine, he could feel it, but he still needed confirmation from the doctor. They were going to spend their life together. She had to be okay. The nurse apologized for the delay and assured him that someone would be out to speak with him shortly.

Tammy jumped up, hoping to hear some news, as Caleb walked back to the waiting area. He didn't say anything; he just shook his head and sat down. His jaws visibly clenched and his temples pulsed as he tried to remain calm. He was being pushed to his limits.

Caleb leaned back in the chair, closed his eyes, and said a silent prayer. He opened his eyes to find a doctor walking into the waiting area. He nearly jumped over chairs to get to the doctor, whom he hoped was there to deliver news about Raegan.

"I'm Raegan's fiancé. How is she doing?" Caleb asked without verifying that he was Raegan's doctor.

"We had to give her a few stitches, but she is recovering well. She's been mumbling your name. The anesthesia is slowly wearing off, so she may be a little disoriented, but otherwise she should be fine," the doctor reported, closing the chart.

"Oh, thank God! Can I see her now?" Caleb pressed.

"Yes, but there is one other thing you must know." The doctor's tone told Caleb that he was about to deliver bad news. Caleb knew what the doctor was referring to before the words even came out of his mouth. He took a deep breath as his shoulders slumped a little and waited for the doctor to say the words.

"The baby did not survive. The trauma was just too much. She started losing the baby before she arrived to the hospital. The force from the collision caused her placenta uterine attachment to detach. At that point, the baby began to lose oxygen. There was nothing we could do by the time she arrived. I'm sorry for your loss," the doctor said.

"I'd like to be with her when you tell her," Caleb said. He knew the news would devastate her. Although she'd been dealing with other issues concerning the baby, he knew that she was very much in love and wanted to have the baby, and so did he. Although they didn't create the child together, he was going to love the baby as though he planted the seed.

Tammy was within earshot, hearing everything that the doctor told Caleb about the baby. She was heartbroken. She wanted to see her but knew that Raegan would need to be with Caleb first. Raegan had always been there for her, so she would do the same. She did the one thing she knew to do—pray. Raegan would need supernatural strength to deal with losing her baby.

The doctor led Caleb to Raegan's recovery room. "I'll give you two a moment and then I will return to speak with her."

"Cami, baby! I'm so glad you're all right! You scared me for a moment there, woman!" Caleb made it to her bedside in three strides. He couldn't wait to hold her in his arms again.

She gave him a weak smile. She was feeling a little incoherent because of the anesthesia, but as the doctor told Caleb, it was beginning to wear off.

"I love you," he professed, planting a kiss on her forehead. He didn't have any other words. He couldn't be the one to break her heart, telling her the baby didn't survive.

"I love you too," she said, sliding up into a sitting position. She thought for a moment, trying to figure out what happened. The last thing she remembered was leaving the coffee shop after talking to Rico and his wife. She was excited that she no longer had to deal with the likes of Rico ever again because he signed over his parental rights. There was no recourse for him; he couldn't show up in their lives later wanting to fight for his rights months or years down the line. He may not have truly wanted to do so, but she was hoping that he would choose repairing his marriage instead of fighting with her over the baby. And she had been right.

It was in that moment that she remembered and tears filled her eyes. She touched her stomach and whispered, "My baby?" She looked into Caleb's eyes to confirm what she knew to be true.

# CHAPTER 18

"Honey, you're late but right on time. My shift is ending so I need you to take over. We have a patient who was involved in a car accident and lost her baby. It's so sad; she doesn't know it yet. The doctor is about to give her the news, but it's time for some pain meds and her vitals check," Chloe's nurse friend updated her and handed her Raegan's chart before walking away.

Chloe was preoccupied with her marital affairs, so she didn't bother to look at the patient's name on the chart before entering the room. She was simply grateful for a distraction—anything right now to take her mind off her lying, adulterous husband.

"Good afternoon," Chloe greeted the patient and her guest as she entered the room. Caleb was sitting in the chair next to Raegan's bed, with his back toward the door. He turned slightly to speak and then returned his attention to Raegan, who couldn't see the nurse because Caleb was blocking her view.

Chloe walked around to the other side of the bed, blood pressure kit in hand, and stopped mid-stride when she got a good look at the patient. There in the bed was Raegan . . . the woman carrying her husband's child . . . well, the one who *had been* carrying his child, according to the nurse who just handed her the chart.

"Oh God!" Raegan whimpered, as her head throbbed and her body stiffened under Caleb's hands. He looked from Raegan to the nurse. Both women were staring at each other as if they'd seen a ghost. Chloe no longer wore the forced friendly smile that was plastered across her face when she entered the room. Her eyes were now narrow and her hands planted on her hips.

"This just *cannot* be happening!" Chloe fumed. *I'll be damned if I give you one painkiller!* Chloe thought. The one thing she was trying to get out of her mind was staring her in the face. As a nurse, Chloe felt a tinge of compassion for Raegan, but she was not about to give her care.

"Babe, what's the matter? What's going on here?" His eyebrows scrunched together as the creases in his forehead formed. Caleb again looked from Raegan to the nurse and could sense the tension, but was confused as to why it was there in the first place.

"Meet Rico's wife—Chloe," Raegan told Caleb, her voice barely above a whisper. She somehow felt that speaking quietly would ease her pain.

Caleb's eyes widened and he looked from one woman to the other, confusion clouding his eyes. He had to have missed something. Under ordinary circumstances he would have extended his hand and offered an *it's nice to meet you,* but that didn't seem appropriate and Chloe didn't seem to be in the mood for introductions.

She snatched Raegan's chart off the counter and stormed out, without ever laying hands on Raegan. As far as she was concerned, her marriage was ending because of Raegan, and her career was not about to go down the drain too. She couldn't help but think that something going wrong with Raegan would be traced back to her and somehow, someone would figure it all out and blame her. Probably a long shot but she wasn't taking a chance. Besides, she wasn't sure she was the one to provide her with the best care. Not in this moment. She was a professional so she knew when to step away.

After nearly tearing the handle off the door to exit, Chloe came face-to-face with the doctor. She shoved the chart into his chest, still seething at the thought that her husband was the father, and walked away, a move she would likely have to answer for later, but she hoped to have her emotions in check by then. She thought Rico fathering another woman's baby was the thing bothering her most, but it wasn't now that she realized Raegan was no longer pregnant. She couldn't be with him again knowing that he shared with Raegan parts of himself that he was only supposed to share with her. She resolved that their marriage had to end whether or not Raegan was still carrying his child. It could no longer work.

∞

Raegan's doctor confirmed her worst fear. This wasn't a nightmare. There was no opening her eyes and things would go back to normal. This was now her reality. She had lost her baby. Just when she felt like she was finally getting a grip on the situation, it slipped through her fingers like sand.

After the doctor gave the bad news, Raegan zoned out. She felt as though losing her baby must have been some sort of consequence for conceiving the baby out of wedlock. She was doing all that she could to correct the situation, but that was not enough. Why would God allow this to happen? The doctor explained that in early pregnancy, the baby is usually protected against such traumas. They likely wouldn't have known that she was pregnant had she not been bleeding; that is when they performed a blood test to detect the presence of hCG. To confirm, they also gave her an ultrasound. Her losing the baby was unfortunate and it was nothing that they could have done since she'd started to lose the baby before arriving at the hospital.

The doctor offered his condolences for their loss and left the room. Caleb saw the look of sorrow on Raegan's face, but he felt helpless. He knew that she had been excited about having the baby and wanted everything to be perfect.

"Cami, we can get through this together. You know I'm right here." Caleb squeezed her hand and planted another kiss on her forehead. He took a seat next to her on the bed and gave her a reassuring hug.

Raegan remained quiet for a while. Caleb didn't want to push her. He was quite unhappy and needed encouragement as well, but he was determined to be strong for her.

"Thank you," Raegan said, her voice faint "Thank you for being here with me. I need this; I need you," she cried, leaning into his embrace. She'd gone from one nightmare to another. The dreams she had of the three of them together would now never be. The doctor assured them that this loss shouldn't affect her being able to carry another child, and she did find comfort in that—the fact that one day she could carry Caleb's baby and they could still have the family they both wanted. There was hope but that didn't erase her sadness.

"I wouldn't be anywhere else." Caleb squeezed her tighter, brushing her curls away from her face and planting another kiss on her forehead.

"I had no doubt about that. Everything is going to be all right, I know, but I still can't believe this is happening . . . after all of the plans we made," Raegan sniffed, remembering the gifts that Caleb recently purchased and her joy at getting Rico out of their lives for good.

"We are still very blessed and I don't think that God loves us any less. He is still awesome in power and His ways are far greater than we know, even when we don't understand," Caleb said, trying to encourage himself as well.

"You're right about that. We'll get through this all right." Raegan sighed and returned his kiss.

"There is someone else here waiting to see you." He knew that having close friends around during times like this would cheer her up. He was thankful that Tammy stopped by.

She slid out of his embrace to see his face. "Who? Did you call someone?"

"No, she called me earlier because she was looking for you. I'll go get her. Be right back." He kissed her again and wiped her tears before walking toward the door. Tammy had been waiting in the hallway since the doctor left the room. Caleb waved her inside.

"I was so worried about you when you didn't answer your phone earlier. I'm so glad that you're all right!" Tammy rushed to her side .and hugged her "I just spoke with Kensi and Michelle. They know that you're doing okay. I told them I would give them an update after I got a chance to see you for myself."

"Thank you so much for coming to see me. How are the plans coming along for the vow renewal?" Raegan changed the subject, no longer wanting to think about her current situation. She saw the look in Tammy's eyes and didn't want her feeling sorry for her. She would much rather talk about something light and exciting.

"They're fine." Ordinarily, Tammy would have shared the issues that she and Joshua were having regarding finances, but she didn't want to talk about that in front of Caleb. She figured that now wasn't the time considering the circumstances. "That is why I was looking for you. I wanted you to come dress shopping with me."

"I'd love it!" Raegan cheered. Finally something that would really keep her mind off her loss. "I should be able to tag along in a couple of days or so. What did you have in mind?" Raegan patted the back of the chair next to the bed.

Caleb walked out of the room to allow them to talk about wedding stuff. He reminded her that he would be right outside the door if she needed him. He could sense that Raegan wanted something else to focus on, but he was still experiencing grief. He also thought they needed to talk about their relationship, but he understood that she needed time. They needed to work on *them* so that they could make their own plans to walk down the aisle. He hoped their loss wouldn't postpone their wedding.

"I had a couple of things in mind, but now I'm thinking of something different. Like custom-design different. It's Joshua's gift to me," Tammy squealed, clasping her hands together in excitement.

"That sounds fancy. A custom-made gown! I love it!" Raegan encouraged. She knew that Tammy often indulged in expensive things, but from the sound of it, Joshua was on board, so there was no reason to caution her about watching her spending.

Tammy kept bridal magazines in her purse to browse through during her free time. She pulled a couple of them out to show Raegan her ideas.

After Caleb left the room, Tammy felt more comfortable talking about her and Joshua's differences when it came to finances. She loved him but didn't want this to become an area of contention in their marriage. She worked hard and definitely didn't want to feel like a prisoner in her marriage. She felt like she should be able to spend whenever she wanted as long as her financial obligations were taken care of.

Raegan agreed with her, but reminded her that she was living as a married woman now and that was something that she and Joshua really needed to discuss. Raegan advised her to talk to Joshua about how she really felt about the issue and try to come to a compromise.

"I've mentioned it a little, but I don't think he understands how much it really bothers me. I mean, it *really* gets under my skin. Does he think I'm going to send him into bankruptcy?" Tammy exaggerated.

"He may not think that, but I'm sure he has his reasons for how he chooses to manage money. You two just have to figure out what works best for your relationship and do that," Raegan reminded her.

Tammy would try to talk to him about it, because she didn't want to continue to hide her spending from him. She felt as if she had to sneak around with spending, and it was eating away at her.

As she and Raegan picked up their conversation about the details of her dress, Tammy kept Raegan's words in the back of her mind. She ran through ways to bring up the situation with Joshua without sounding confrontational.

She loved him and she wanted their marriage to work this time around, so she was committed to doing all that she could do to make that happen. First thing on her list was to get this money situation straightened out, no matter how difficult the conversation was going to be.

# CHAPTER 19

Although Raegan was down about losing her baby, she also felt some sort of relief. And then she felt guilty about *that*. Rico was out of her life for good and she would have no constant reminder of how she allowed herself to get caught up in his lies. She loved the baby no matter the circumstances surrounding the conception, but if she were to be honest, she despised Rico for his lies and the false hope he'd given to her. She was even more disappointed in herself for falling for them.

Caleb watched Raegan roam aimlessly around the kitchen. He knew that something must have been bothering her because she'd opened and closed the refrigerator door at least five times and hadn't put anything in or taken anything out. She was distracted and he was certain it had something to do with the accident, whether it was losing the baby or working with the insurance company for a new car, since her car was totaled.

The accident happened more than a week ago and they hadn't really talked much about it or the baby. He'd come by to check on her every day and she hadn't said much about the loss, although he knew it was bothering her. Caleb walked into the kitchen, grasped Raegan's hand, and led her to the living area to sit down and talk. It was as if a thick cloud was hovering over them, and it was high time they removed it.

"Talk to me, Cami. What's going on inside of your pretty little head?" Caleb asked, placing a kiss on her temple as he snuggled her closer to him on his lap.

Raegan nestled her head into his chest. "I keep going over the accident and everything that happened afterwards. It was my fault. All of it. If I hadn't been fumbling around with my cell phone, I would still be carrying our baby. If I'd never called Rico, I would have never spoken with his wife and the meeting would have never happened. Maybe God is punishing me somehow for demanding that Rico give up his paternity rights."

Raegan had not yet discussed where she was before the accident happened or her meeting with Rico and his wife. She almost forgot that fact until she felt Caleb stiffen at her mention of

Rico's parental rights. She knew that he was conflicted about the situation and only wanted what was best for everyone involved. They had also agreed that they would handle it together but all of that changed when she made that phone call to Rico and his wife answered.

Caleb treaded lightly. In a gentle tone, he asked, "Is that where you were before the accident?" He rubbed her fingers as he awaited her response, his cheek resting against hers. He knew the answer. He just wanted confirmation. He didn't want her handling the situation with Rico alone mostly because he knew that she would become easily frazzled, causing stress to both her and the baby. And since they were in it together, he needed to be there; they were a team. He also believed that his presence would eliminate any confusion with Chloe in regards to Raegan's intentions. Raegan was with him now and it was up to Chloe how she handled her marriage.

"Yes, that's where I was. I'm sorry I didn't tell you about it beforehand. I was actually calling to tell Rico about the baby when his wife answered the phone. She was curious about why I called her husband and I didn't want to lie to her. Too many lies have been told already. We met. We talked....well I did most of the talking. She then called Rico to confront him. He joined us and I did what I thought was best at the time to get him out of our lives for good – having him sign over his parental rights so that he couldn't come back and try to fight for custody one day. After he signed the papers, I left the two of them in the coffee shop. That is when I called to tell you what happened and I dropped my phone. The rest is history." After her quick recount of the events she let out a sigh of relief.

Caleb pondered her words for a while. Raegan's attempting to take matters into her own hands again frustrated him. But nothing could be done about that now. They had no baby to fight over and now it seemed they could move on without Rico in their lives. He knew she thought she was doing the right thing even if he didn't agree with her. But now, none of that mattered any longer.

"I see." Switching the subject, he said, "I have a buyer for my home, so I'm flying back to Atlanta in a few days for the closing. Cami, why don't you come with me? It'll be nice to have a change of scenery. Don't you think?" He gently squeezed her again and placed a kiss on her temple as he waited for her answer.

"That's very sweet of you and I actually agree, but I probably should be getting back to work." Raegan snuggled closer to him. His arms wrapped around her gave her unspeakable comfort. "I'll be here waiting for you when you return. How long will you be away?"

"Just a couple of days. I'm going to work at the office there and maybe hang out with some of my old coworkers." He was hesitant about leaving her alone though, so he pressed a little. "Are you sure you don't want to come with me?"

"I'll be just fine. I have plenty of things to keep me busy. My work is piling up for sure," she said, gesturing to her work phone that seemed to constantly beep from incoming e-mails.

Caleb relented. He understood she needed things to return to normal, but he wanted to make sure that she didn't fall into some sort of depression. She was putting on a brave face but was finding the loss hard.

After talking for a while longer, he returned to the home that they would soon share and packed up a few of his things for his trip. He reminded himself that he needed to contact Tammy to check in on Raegan for him while he was away. Even though it would only be a couple of days, he still needed assurance that she was doing well. He couldn't bear the thought of losing her. He'd lost her once and had come close to losing her for good. He had to do everything in his power to protect her.

∞

Caleb stopped by his old home one last time to walk through it and ponder the changes in his life. He was getting a second chance to be with his love. He reflected on the good times he'd had in his home but thought more about all the great things to come in the home he purchased for himself and Raegan back in Houston.

As he walked around the house, accompanied by his thoughts, the doorbell rang. He was confused as to who would be ringing his doorbell midday, especially since he'd moved away. No one knew he was there. He figured it must have been a sales person or Jehovah's Witness.

Caleb answered the door to find Natalie, his ex-girlfriend, with a little boy who appeared to be about a year old in her arms. Caleb and Natalie had ended their relationship nearly two years before and they hadn't been in contact since. Now here she was holding a little boy who, if Caleb didn't know any better, looked a lot like him.

# CHAPTER 20

Time seemed to stop for Caleb as he stood in the doorway looking from the child to Natalie and back to the child again. The resemblance was striking. He remembered pictures he'd seen of himself as a child and the little boy's face mirrored his. He was rendered speechless. He wasn't expecting to see Natalie again. And he definitely wasn't expecting her to show up on his doorpost with a child in tow.

Natalie spoke first. "I heard you were moving to Texas."

Caleb nodded, watching the two of them as he stood in the doorway with his hands tucked away in his pockets.

"I thought you should meet Nicholas before you left," she said as her gaze shifted to the child in her arms.

Caleb continued to gaze at Nicholas and waited for her to confirm that Nicholas was his son.

"I know we haven't spoken since the break-up and I've debated the issue with myself over and over again," she began, shifting from one foot to the other. "Even though things didn't work out between us, I couldn't keep this precious little guy away from you," she declared, nuzzling Nicholas' neck.

Just as Caleb thought his life was getting less complicated, it was actually becoming more intricate. Natalie was acting as if she was doing him some sort of favor, but Caleb thought differently.

In a matter of seconds, he went from confused to furious to excited. Why had she been so selfish all of this time? How could she keep his son away from him? *Wasn't that the same thing Raegan was planning to do to Rico?* his conscience yelled at him.

But this was different. Very different. Rico was married and he at least knew about the child. Raegan gave him a choice to give up his parental rights. It probably wasn't much of a choice but at least he had an option.

Caleb had missed at least a year of this precious child's life all because of Natalie. Caleb invited them in and reached for Nicholas, whose arms went happily flailing into the air. It was as if he knew that was where he should be—in his father's arms.

Caleb loved the idea of being a father, but although the child looked like him, in the back of his mind he wondered if Nicholas was really his. One of the many reasons that he and Natalie split was that she was unfaithful to him.

"Why did you wait so long to tell me I had a child?" he inquired through a clenched-teeth smile, never taking his eyes off Nicholas. He sat down and bounced him up and down on his knee.

"I was upset with you for not giving us another chance, so I wanted to hurt you." She gave the partial truth. She wanted him to hurt, but she also wasn't really sure if the baby was his when she learned she was pregnant. Looking at him now, she was sure that Nicholas was his son, although she never had a paternity test done with either of the other two potential fathers.

"So how long were you planning to withhold him from me? Why now?" he continued to question her.

"Like I said, I heard you were moving away. What were the chances of me seeing you again? Would you rather I showed up in Houston five years from now interrupting your happily married life?"

Caleb stood and walked over to her, appalled at her suggestion. "Absolutely not! I would have liked to have known the moment you knew! How about that Nat? How could you keep my son away from me?" The news of Nicholas combined with his pent-up frustration over Raegan losing her baby nearly sent Caleb into a frenzy.

It was too late for all of that now though. Now that he was moving away, how were they going to work out visitation arrangements?

"How do you figure we work this out since I'm leaving? When am I going to see him?" he fussed.

Natalie remained silent and shrugged her shoulders. She couldn't tell him the entire story. She couldn't share everything all in one day; it would just be too much to digest. And at this point, he probably wouldn't believe her if she told him about her situation now. Because of her lies and deception in the past, he'd conclude that she was up to no good. So for now, she'd let him rejoice in the fact that Nicholas was his son. Besides, who could resist his chubby little cheeks and cheery smile?

Caleb tickled Nicholas, enjoying the sound of his giggles. This was just what he wanted with Raegan. Yes, Raegan. For a split-second, he'd forgotten about their situation. How was he going to break this news to her? How would she take it? It would break her heart. She just lost a child and hardly had time to grieve, and then he walks through the door telling her that he now has one.

Raegan loved him, so she'd understand and help him work out a solution to see Nicholas, he mused. He knew that she was still hurting, so he'd have to break the news to her gently. He wanted to give her time to heal from their loss, but didn't want to let too much time pass without sharing the truth.

Caleb put Nicholas back into his mother's arms as he gathered his briefcase so that he could head to the office. He made arrangements to see Nicholas again before he left town the next day. They also made plans to have a DNA test. He couldn't go back to his fiancée telling her about a child without the DNA results. He felt a twinge of guilt just thinking about the word DNA. Recently, he was upset with Raegan for wanting a paternity test and now *he* is the one wanting one. *Life sure does know how to give you a taste of your own medicine,* he thought.

It was hard letting go of the child even though he had held him for just a few moments. He wanted that with Raegan and was sure that she wanted it with him. Now he just had to find a way to tell her that they were going to have it sooner than later—just not in the way they thought they would.

# CHAPTER 21

Raegan went to work but couldn't quite concentrate for thoughts of having lost her baby. After all she had gone through from getting paternity tests to having Rico give up his parental rights, it had turned out to be for nothing. Her spirit was low. She didn't have any words to pray except for, "Help me Lord." That had to be enough. She needed it to be enough because she was so consumed with hurt.

She was in such a slump that she took personal time for the rest of the day. She needed time to refresh so that she could fully focus on her newly assigned tasks because of her promotion. She realized that the pregnancy and everything that came along with it had consumed her for the past couple of weeks.

Tears filled her eyes as she mindlessly drove back to her house. She nearly rear-ended a vehicle that came to a sudden stop in front of her. That quickly jolted her back to reality and quietly reminded her of how she lost her baby in the first place—not paying much attention to what was going on in front of her. She was thankful that her insurance company replaced her old car with a newer model equipped with brake assist, Bluetooth, navigation and a rear camera.

Determined to focus on the road, she answered her telephone on the car's Bluetooth when it rang. Hearing Tammy's jubilant voice through the speakers, she smiled. Tammy had been checking up on her quite a bit since Caleb left, almost to the point where Raegan was becoming annoyed.

"I just called your office and couldn't reach you. Where are you going?"

"Home," Raegan answered without any explanation.

"Joshua and I just came back from the hospital. He's going to the house to relax, but I'm certainly free. Are you up for company, girlfriend?"

"I suppose," murmured Raegan. Tammy's mind was mostly filled with wedding stuff these days, with her vow renewal ceremony drawing closer. That would help take Raegan's mind off of everything for a while. She'd spoken to Caleb and was happy to know that he would be returning tomorrow.

"Great, I'll meet you at your house," Tammy said before clicking off the line.

By the time Raegan pressed the button to open her garage door, Tammy was pulling into the driveway behind her. Tammy did just as Caleb had asked of her—check-in on Raegan and make sure that she wasn't sulking around. Raegan had been there for her when she lost her grandmother and she vowed to do the same for her now.

"Hello *bestest* friend in the state of Texas." Tammy walked toward Raegan with her arms stretched wide.

"Just Texas? Usually people say the world," Raegan chided, leaning in to Tammy's embrace.

"I knew that would get your attention! Of course you're the best in the world," Tammy said, looping her arm in Raegan's as they walked into the house.

"So how are you really doing?" Tammy inquired.

Raegan sat down in her recliner and let out a long sigh. All she knew was that her heart hurt and she wanted this all behind her. She needed to move on but couldn't quite figure out how.

"I don't know. My heart is broken or maybe it's been ripped from my chest. I feel like someone dangled a treat in front of me and snatched it away. Imagine receiving an award that you knew you didn't deserve but yet it was given to you anyway, only for you to walk away and break it. Boom! It's gone. It's like it was never there. You have no proof of the undeserved gift. You cannot get it back—not that one anyway."

"Can I share something with you?" Tammy asked, pulling out her phone and opening the Bible app. Without an answer from a dazed Raegan, she began reading Psalm 127:3, "Children are a gift from the Lord; they are a reward from him."

Raegan frowned a little but that is exactly what she would have done if the situation were reversed. However, that Scripture did not make her feel any better. In fact, it made her feel worse; because if children were a gift from God, that also meant that God had taken the gift back. Why He would do that or allow that to happen to her, she just couldn't understand.

"Now I know what you're thinking and you can't beat yourself up about this. God is sovereign and all powerful. If He gave that child to you, we both know that He can do it again. You just need to have faith and believe that it is somehow working together for your good."

*But where was the good in that? Being rid of Rico?* she thought. She didn't utter the words to Tammy because Tammy had just as many answers as she did, and that meant none. Raegan was grateful for the soft chime of the doorbell, although she had no idea who that could be this time of day. Curious, she went to the door, squinted through the peephole and let out a soft squeal when she got a glimpse of the person standing on the other side of the door.

"Kensi!" Raegan cheered, flinging open the door. "What are you doing here?" Raegan pulled her friend into a tight squeeze.

"I had a layover at Hobby Airport and I had to take that opportunity to check on you. There is no way you're going through this without me by your side honey!" Kensi exclaimed, holding up a gift basket filled with Raegan's favorite snacks and lotions that she picked up on her way to Raegan's house. She called Tammy when her flight landed to confirm Raegan's whereabouts. Raegan leaving work early fit perfectly into Kensi's plan to visit.

Raegan pulled her inside and showed her off to Tammy as if she were a prize. "Look who's here!"

Tammy joined in the excitement and hugged Kensi; she was grateful because she now had some reinforcement. Raegan offered Kensi water and snacks before taking a seat on the sofa. Kensi plopped down next to Raegan, linked her fingers in hers and chimed right in with the same line of questioning that Tammy started. She was concerned about her friend and was determined to make sure she did everything in her power to reassure her that things would be all right.

"Thanks for coming Kens. It's so good to have you here." Raegan rested her head on Kensi's shoulder.

"Don't mention it," Kensi replied with a wave of her free hand. "This is 9-1-1. You have to know that your girls are here for you."

"You know we are always here for you Raegan. I've been praying for you. I had thirty-something years on this earth with my grandma and I can only imagine what you must feel not being able to get to know your baby at all. Just know that in time, you will be able to get past this. Time helps us heal," Tammy continued. "I believe that you will have tons of babies running around here and you will be able to share your story of loss and healing to help someone else. Because whether you know it or not, you helped me—beginning with praying for my family in the hospital. And I think that is one of the best things that we can do for you right now."

Tammy got up and sat on the other side of Raegan, grabbed her slippery palm, and began to pray, "Heavenly Father, thank You for being almighty. We know that Your thoughts are much higher than our thoughts and Your ways are much better than ours. You see what's to come before we do and we believe by faith that You have our best interests at heart."

Kensi picked up in prayer where Tammy left off. "Many women were presented to us in the Bible as examples of your almighty power. Barren. Old. And yet, You still showed them favor and allowed them to bear children. We know that it was so that Your power could be demonstrated. And we believe in that same power. Power to heal hearts. Power to make barren wombs fertile. Power to give Raegan and Caleb all of the children they desire if it be Your will. So now in Jesus' name, we ask in faith that You comfort both Raegan and Caleb as they deal with this transition in their lives and help them to know that You are still God and You are the One from whom all blessings flow. In Jesus' powerful name we pray, Amen."

"Thank you so much." Raegan hugged her friends. "I hope y'all plan to babysit all these kids y'all praying for me to have," said Raegan through a smile and tear-stained face. She was grateful to have friends of faith who could step in and pray for her even when she was so broken-hearted that she couldn't pray for herself. She felt an overwhelming sense of peace. Everything was going to be all right. She knew it. Maybe she and Caleb could start working on their first child as soon as they were married. She was sure he would like that very much. And so would she.

# CHAPTER 22

Joshua found it rather difficult getting through their counseling session with thoughts of the ten-thousand-dollar bill for Tammy's dress. Sure, he told her that it was his gift to her, but he figured she'd go as far as two thousand dollars—three at the most—but ten thousand!

When Tammy accepted his proposal to reconcile, they decided it would be a good idea to go through marriage counseling sessions in order to prevent them from splitting again, if at all possible. Seeing as though he couldn't quite get Tammy on board with managing her spending, or at least understanding how important it was to him, marriage counseling was definitely in order. Someone had to help him get through to her.

Joshua was snapped back into the present when their marriage counselor, Reverend Thomas Wright, called out to him.

"Are you all right there, son?" Rev. Wright asked, peering over his bifocals. His salt-and-pepper goatee reminded Joshua of a younger and slimmer T. D. Jakes.

"Yes, sir. I'm sorry, I didn't get the question," Joshua stammered a little.

Tammy touched his knee. She could tell that something was bothering him. He had been quiet since she announced that she had the perfect dress and the planning was complete. She thought he would be thrilled with her proclamation but instead she got the feeling that he wasn't pleased.

Rev. Wright eyed Joshua carefully as he spoke on the issue of differences. He knew that something was eating at him and decided that he would address it before their session ended.

"As I was saying, no two people are the same and often opposites do attract. You need to know that it is okay to be different, not only physically but also in thought. Our backgrounds, the way we were raised and our outlook on life affect our behavior and the way we see things. It is important that you two take time to discuss children and how you will handle finances . . . " Rev. Wright continued on but noticed something change in Joshua's demeanor when he mentioned finances.

As someone who had financial issues in his marriage early on, Rev. Wright thought he should address the issue with the couple now. Even though that issue was scheduled to be discussed a few sessions down the line, he couldn't help but notice that it was currently an area of contention between the couple.

"What is the money issue?" Rev. Wright asked bluntly.

Tammy looked from Joshua to the Reverend. *How did he know there was an issue?* she wondered.

Joshua took the initiative to answer Rev. Wright's question. Since the moment he checked his bank account and noticed the extraordinary amount of money Tammy spent on her dress, he had been disappointed. He was actually glad that they were about to discuss this now, because he wasn't sure if he could hold on to it any longer. They needed the presence of an unbiased third party who could help Tammy see things his way.

"Reverend, it's like this." Joshua scooted to the edge of his seat, leaned forward and explained his side of things. "I'm thinking about our future and the future of our soon-to-be children. I don't think we should spend money on expensive things just because we can afford to do so. I wouldn't feel any differently if I had one thousand dollars in the bank as opposed to several million," he answered, shifting his eyes toward Tammy.

Without giving the reverend any time to comment, Tammy defended her spending. "It's not as if I'm not concerned about our future, but what is a few thousand dollars spent here and there when we have millions? That's not going to hurt anything. He's acting as if he thinks I'm going to blow *his* money and send him into bankruptcy." Squinting at Joshua she said, "I know you've worked hard to get where you are. I'm not trying to take that from you. Have you forgotten that I work and I'm very well able to take care of myself? Haven't I turned down your offers to *help* me over the years?" Her chest was heaving and slightly irritated from the finger she'd been pressing against her chest while trying to make her point.

Joshua remained silent because he felt as if Tammy still didn't quite understand his point. It wasn't that he didn't think they should purchase nice things; he was just of the mindset that they needed to be reasonable. Having a budget, and sticking to it, was important to him. He'd seen far too many athletes go bankrupt and he wasn't about to lose his mind and become one of them.

Taking the silence as his cue to intervene, the Reverend asked, "So how do you think your finances should be handled in marriage?" His eyes darted between the two of them. They glared at each other as if to say they weren't budging on their perspectives.

Seeing that they weren't making any progress on the topic, Reverend Wright said, "I can't give you the answer, but what I can tell you is that the wrong way to enter into this reconciliation is with the *I* and *my* mentality. You both have to understand that when you come together, it becomes *our* and *we*. So I'm going to give you an assignment. When you return for your next session, I want to know your stance on finances in regards to tithing, budgeting, emergency savings, joint accounts, and spending. I also want to discuss what your thoughts are regarding who should manage the finances."

Reverend Wright shared the issues he and his wife faced when they first married. Hiding credit cards. Hiding purchases. Dealing with debt created before and after their vows. They had very little guidance before they married and it almost ruined their marriage. He always made sure to address the issue with young couples during his counseling sessions. He knew how disastrous it could be and always worked to help couples avoid money issues by discussing them up front.

"Should we work on this together, or do you want us to work on it separately and discuss it with you when we come back?" Tammy asked.

Rev. Wright thought for a moment then said, "Let's do this. Work on it separately and then come together and discuss what you have with one another before coming back next week. How does that sound?" He felt like a school teacher issuing homework.

"Use this booklet as a guide." Reverend Wright handed them a thick booklet he used in financial seminars hosted on weekends at his church.

"We can handle that," Joshua spoke for both of them as he took the document Reverend Wright insisted they use. He knew they had a long way to go, but he was glad to finally get a chance to discuss the issue weighing so heavily on him on neutral grounds.

Tammy nodded in agreement. She knew the purchase of the wedding dress must have sent his blood pressure through the roof. She knew it was a bit over the top, but he said it would be his gift to her. She didn't think he would be crying about it during counseling. Now that it was out in the open, hopefully they could work this out so that she wouldn't have to hear about it every time she swiped her debit card.

# CHAPTER 23

The moment Caleb laid eyes on Raegan again, his world shifted. He fell deeper in love with her than he ever thought possible. The mere thought of having her again excited him, and that became a reality when she agreed to marry him. A long-awaited dream come true, but with a baby who wasn't his. He loved her, so he could love the baby. He was sure that he would love the baby as his own. But he knew Raegan well enough to know that if things didn't fit in her perfect little world, she would have nothing to do with it. And Nicholas was not part of that perfect world. But Raegan loved him, and with time he was sure she could accept the little boy. How much time? He wasn't certain; so he would wait to tell her until he thought she was ready. He didn't want to begin their new life together keeping secrets, but he felt like these were special circumstances.

As promised, Caleb contacted Natalie to spend time with Nicholas before he left town. But before they went on their outing, Caleb met Natalie and Nicholas at the hospital, where they had the DNA test performed. He could have been convinced that Nicholas was his biological son by looking at him; Nicholas was a spitting image of Caleb. However, he would need more proof than just looks before he took on the role of father and before he told Raegan. The results wouldn't be available for a few days, but unfortunately, he was getting ready to leave town. He didn't want them mailed for fear that Raegan would somehow find the letter. He decided that he would get the results when he returned.

After taking care of their business at the hospital, Caleb took Nicholas to the children's museum. They played at the different stations, starting from the science lab and going to the restaurant kitchen, from the space center to the sporting area, then to the supermarket, and finally to the playground. Both Caleb and Nicholas enjoyed every minute of it. An hour and a half later, Nicholas was wiped out, snoring in the backseat. Caleb had planned to grab something to eat with him, but that was out since Nicholas was tired and already asleep. Spending time with Nicholas felt natural, almost as if he'd been doing it all of Nicholas' life.

Nicholas was still a little boy and probably had no idea what they were getting into, but he enjoyed every moment. Caleb relished the giggles, squeals and little arms wrapped around his neck throughout the day. He wished he could experience that joy with Raegan. In fact, he knew she could use it right about now.

∞

Caleb sat on the plane, eyes closed, headphones on, signaling that he didn't want to be neighborly. His thoughts danced around his head during his return flight to Houston. He had a lot on his mind and he needed to figure out how he would bring this up to Raegan, and when. He knew it would have to wait, but he needed a plan. After all that he and Raegan had just gone through, how was he going to tell her that he possibly had a child?

Part of him still needed answers from Natalie. *Why would she keep something like this from me? Who is raising my son?* His mind raced. *But weren't you going to do the same thing to Rico? Raise his child as your own?* His thoughts betrayed him. *This is different. Rico gave up his rights; I never got the chance to make any choice. My choice was taken away.*

He pulled out his cellphone to look at the pictures he took of Nicholas. That one-year-old, six-tooth smile warmed his heart. He smiled at the memories that he'd already begun to create with Nicholas. He had only known about him for a couple of days and

Nicholas had instantly stolen his heart. He hated that he wasn't there during his first months of life.

Caleb heard the flight attendant over the intercom telling the passengers to lift their tray tables and return their seats to an upright position. He let out a long, hard sigh. What was possibly one of the best moments in his life had to be kept a secret. Well, it didn't have to be—he could give Raegan a chance, but he knew her. He couldn't risk her running away again. He had to find a way to ease her into this.

As the plane made its final descent into Houston, Caleb's mind plowed through a plethora of excuses and reasoning on why he couldn't tell Raegan the truth.

Seated in first class, Caleb was one of the first passengers to get off the plane. Grateful he had packed only a carry-on bag, he quickly maneuvered through the airport terminal to the passenger pick-up area. Perfect timing. Raegan pulled up to the waiting area and jumped out of the car to greet him.

The moment they were close enough, he lifted her by the waist, pulling her into his arms, and kissed her as if it would be the last time. She missed him, too, so she thought nothing of the grand kiss.

"I missed you, beautiful," Caleb said as he lowered her. Seeing her made his day just as much as it had made hers.

"I missed you," she murmured against his lips, sliding against his frame until her feet touched the ground.

Caleb eyed the guard nearing Raegan's car to ask them to move the vehicle. Before the guard could say a word, they hopped into the car, with Caleb in the driver's seat, and drove away.

Raegan shifted her slender frame in the passenger seat so that she was facing Caleb. On the ride to Caleb's house, they chatted about wedding planning. They were in agreement that they should begin looking forward to their future. Raegan's face lit up as they discussed their wedding and possibly starting a family soon after. She was so caught up in their chatter that she hardly noticed the wrinkles in Caleb's forehead.

He knew he had to do something about this paternity situation soon because his choice to delay sharing the details with Raegan was already eating at him and it had only been a few days. A few days too long. He loved her and he knew he couldn't keep it from her for long. If she found out on her own, she would likely never forgive him. There was no way she would see it from his point of view.

She would only see betrayal.

# CHAPTER 24

Raegan and Caleb arrived at the house that would soon be their home. Raegan walked through the living room and into the kitchen. The perfect idea hit her as she peered through the French glass doors leading to the backyard. She spun around to meet Caleb's gaze as he smiled down at her. By the look on her face, he could tell that her wheels had begun turning.

"I know that face. What are you thinking?" he asked.

"What do you think about an outdoor wedding?" She smiled as she bit her bottom lip in anticipation of his response.

"And by outdoor, you mean…here?" he asked as he pointed toward the backyard. It was more of a statement than a question. He thought for a moment as he walked closer to her, spinning her around to face the outdoors. "Let's think about that for a minute," he said, wrapping his arms around her and kissing her gently on the ear.

"Backyard wedding! That sounds funny I know, but work with me here. Think about it. We have plenty of yard space. The scenery is already set. We just need decorations, tents and someone to put down hardwood flooring for the dance floor."

"I like the idea of an outside wedding, but I don't know about having the wedding at our house. We need to think about that for a while," he cautioned, reminding her about the downside of hosting events at home. Clean-up. Kicking people out. Boundaries.

"I suppose that does require more thought," she spoke softly. She then remembered how difficult it was to bring home parties to an end. No one ever wanted to leave. She thought it would be a great way to celebrate their new lives together with the new house and wedding celebration all in one. *But maybe that isn't the best idea,* she thought.

"But if that's your vision and you're sold on it, I can deal with having a wedding at home and having all of our friends and family over for one day."

"Are you sure?" she asked, leaning into his chest as she imagined how the event would turn out with so many people in their home. He read her mind because that was exactly what she'd been thinking.

"Like I said before . . . anything to see that beautiful smile of yours. Well, let me clarify that. Anything within reason," he said and chuckled.

"I'm going to hold you to that in more ways than one," she said, breaking the embrace and pulling him by the hand to the kitchen island to sit.

Caleb was glad to see Raegan in a better mood and he hoped that he had something to do with it. Losing the baby proved to be more heartbreaking than he'd ever thought possible. How was he going to tell her about Nicholas? He decided to test the waters just to see where she stood on the children issue. They had never really talked about it in detail. Still holding onto her hands, he opened the subject for discussion.

"Cami, how soon are you willing to get pregnant again?" He hoped it wasn't too soon to bring it up, but he wanted to see where her feelings were.

"Where did that come from? Are you trying to tell me that you want to start trying as soon as we get married?" She wondered if he thought that working on another baby would help her get over their recent loss.

"We don't necessarily have to actively try, but we don't have to do anything to prevent it in any way, if that's okay with you. You have to do most of the work, so I'll leave that up to you; we can try as soon as you feel ready."

"Okay, let me think about that for a while. I haven't given it much thought considering what happened," her voice trailed off as the images of losing her baby flashed through her mind.

"You know, Cami, we've never really discussed your feelings about losing the baby. Tell me . . . how are you dealing with that? You haven't really talked to me about it," Caleb said as he tugged on the barstool where she sat, pulling her closer to him. He wanted her to know that she could talk to him about anything. Even that.

Raegan sighed as she pondered his question. She'd been trying to deal with it in her own way. Alone. Although Caleb said he would treat the child as his own, a part of her felt awkward sharing her loss with him since the child wasn't his biologically.

"You know honey . . . I'm okay. I think I've had enough time to grieve. The doctor assured me that the accident does not affect me carrying another child," she said as she rubbed her belly. "I feel terrible for even thinking this, but not having Rico's baby assures me that I no longer have to deal with any part of him. Losing the baby broke my heart, but knowing that I'll never have to deal with him in any way gives me a sense of peace." She bowed her head to hide the shame she felt for thinking and revealing her true feelings.

She had not really discussed how it made her feel to know that the child she was carrying belonged to Rico. Although she already loved her baby, she couldn't deny that the baby would be a constant reminder of all the things that went wrong in her life with Rico. Fornication. Adultery. Lies. She was glad to be rid of him even if that meant losing her baby. She truly felt bad for thinking that, but it was the truth.

"Come here," Caleb said, lifting her from the barstool and pulling her onto his lap. "Don't forget that you have me to lean on. I don't ever want you holding something like that inside. While it's true that Rico betrayed you, you can't hold on to the hurt. I love you and I hope that's enough to help you through the pain. We're finally getting ready to have the life we wanted. You and me. And many babies," he chuckled.

She playfully pushed him away at the sound of "many babies."

"I didn't say all of that. A couple. Not many." She smiled and pulled him close for a kiss. Not missing a beat, he returned the kiss, thankful that the elephant was out of the room. Now if only he could tell her about Nicholas. Seeing she seemed to still be in a tender place, he chose to keep it to himself. Now still wasn't the best time.

# CHAPTER 25

"You just want to control me!" Tammy screamed at Joshua. She was getting fed up arguing with him about money. Although they managed to collaborate on the assignment Reverend Wright had given to them, their issues still hadn't been resolved.

"Why does this have to be so difficult, woman?" Joshua said, equally frustrated but without elevating his voice as Tammy had. He rubbed his hands over his face trying to keep his cool as much as possible.

"Excuse me? Look around you, Josh!" She twirled slowly. "I think I have managed to do quite well with money so far. You're standing in a house that I purchased by myself. I didn't ask you or anyone else for anything!"

"I never said you haven't managed your money well, Tammy." Joshua plopped down on the couch and rubbed his temples. He was tired of having the same argument with her. She never wanted to listen because she was so caught up on the notion that he wanted to control her.

"You may not have said it directly, but you say it every single time we have this conversation. You're starting to sound like a broken record," she said through clenched teeth.

"And you're acting like a selfish teenager! That's the Tammy I know. Always wanting things her way. Never wanting to listen to anyone. That is why we separated in the first place!" The words slipped out of his mouth before he could catch himself. He'd been holding back his feelings regarding their separation for a long time. He never wanted to shift all the blame onto her for their failed relationship, but right now she was pushing his buttons. *Why can't she see that I only want what's best for our family? Our future? If something ever happened to me, I want to make sure that she is well taken care of for years to come,* he thought to himself. "You're so self-centered!"

"What did you say?" Tammy spun around. "How dare you? I wasn't the only selfish one in our relationship. Don't you dare blame me!" Tammy's voice remained elevated.

Joshua's words lit a fire in Tammy and their arguing escalated, each of them throwing stones from their past. Joshua had never expressed how much their separation hurt him, but in Tammy's defense, she didn't believe that it bothered him much since he never did much to mend their relationship.

"Oh yeah! You were selfish and you know it!"

"Well I guess that makes two of us! You knew how to find me, but wait, basketball was your one true love, right?"

"Didn't you ever think for one moment that I needed you, my wife, by my side? But what did you do? Run off to Texas!" He stood and closed the gap between them; his voice was now raised, matching her tone. He pointed to the floor next to him to emphasize his point as his nose flared and eyes tightened.

*Needed me?* Tammy never considered that Joshua needed her and he certainly never told her that. She presumed that basketball was all he needed since that was all he pursued after she left. Her arms dropped from her hips in surrender and her eyes became misty. *So me leaving is really what this is all about?*

"Wait, I'm sorry. We're getting off topic and all of this screaming back and forth is not going to help us solve the problem," he said gently and in a much quieter tone when he noticed her defeated stance and the tears welling up in her eyes. He wasn't trying to hurt her with his words. He remembered the Bible verse that he'd been studying all week, Proverbs 15:1: *A gentle answer turns away wrath but a harsh word stirs up anger*. He was intent on being the peacemaker in this situation because he needed her to see where he was coming from. And his mission was definitely not to control her or make her feel guilty over what happened in their past.

"Please sit," he commanded. Joshua pulled her onto the sofa in front of him, his legs on either side of her.

Joshua caressed Tammy's arms, nuzzled his head into her neck and apologized for bringing up past hurts, especially since they agreed they would move on. Tammy stopped him because she didn't realize he felt that way. The truth of the matter is that she had been very selfish when it came to their marriage and he had every right to release his pent-up frustration. There was no way he would have held that in forever; better now than later.

After sorting through unresolved feelings, they still had to come to an agreement on their money issues. Joshua spoke gently, not wanting another argument, explaining his desire for them to have a budget and what that looked like to him—allocating money to give to church, savings, bills, and miscellaneous spending or what he liked to call play money. He turned her attention to the spreadsheet he had begun to build on his laptop. He thought she would be able to understand his point of view a lot better if she could see the numbers.

Tammy thought about the circumstances surrounding Joshua's health. She understood his concern and his need to make sure that everything was in place just in case something went terribly wrong.

Sitting down talking through it made Tammy realize that Joshua didn't have an *I'm the man, do what I say* attitude. She actually agreed with him after going over his spreadsheet, but she knew there would have to be some compromise. She didn't want to go crazy, but since they could afford certain things, she planned to make sure that she had access to them: regular spa treatments, trips, and luxury cars. Surely that wasn't too much to ask.

∞

After several hours of that gruesome but much needed discussion, Joshua placed the laptop aside and carried Tammy to their bedroom, gently placing her into the center of the bed.

"There's something else we need to talk about, sweetheart," Joshua said between planting kisses on her neck. Tammy rolled her eyes. She'd had enough serious discussion for the night.

"And that would be?"

"Babies," Joshua whispered into her ear after kissing it. He ended his shower of kisses to get a good look at her. She was no doubt tired, but the glimmer in her eyes was unmistakable.

"Really?" She raised up on her elbows and lifted her head to kiss him. Now that was something she could talk about and was, in fact, ready to discuss. Lately, he had been so consumed with his bank account that she didn't even want to bring up the topic of starting a family.

Joshua nodded and positioned himself to sit on the bed, pulling Tammy into a sitting position as well, so that she was facing him. Joshua's heart danced in his chest as he awaited a more definite response from her.

Tammy was ready. However, she needed to think about her career. When they agreed that Joshua would recover in Texas, they also agreed that he would allow her to move forward in her career and that he would support her in that; she wasn't sure how a baby would affect her career mobility, although she looked forward to having little Joshuas and Tammys running around. But then there was his heart condition. *Would I have to worry about our children having a heart condition too?* That thought alone overwhelmed her.

Joshua waved his hand in front of Tammy's face because she seemed to be having the conversation in her mind. "Babe, are you with me?"

"Oh, yeah, sorry. I like the sound of 'babies.'" She gave a toothy grin and pulled him in for a kiss.

"Umm, so does that mean you're ready to start? With a kiss like that, please tell me you're ready," he groaned, his face about an inch away from hers.

"Practice makes perfect," she answered and lowered his head to hers as she lay down on the bed. She wanted babies but she also wanted her career. That would have to be one more hurdle they needed to cross before they could live their happily ever after.

# CHAPTER 26

Raegan and Caleb had begun planning the backyard wedding, but the details were becoming overwhelming to a point where they decided to scratch the idea and allow the professionals to handle it. They could only imagine what their wedding day would be like if it mirrored the chaotic planning. That idea was nice in theory, but there was no way they could manage keeping their house in order and getting people to leave when it was time. La Tranquila Ranch became their venue of choice—giving them everything they wanted for their special day without the hassle of having the wedding and reception in their own backyard. For Raegan, having the ceremony in a church was out of the question. Raegan was relieved when she and Caleb came to that agreement—the last thing she wanted was to relive memories of walking down the aisle to Damian in the church and every moment after. A fresh atmosphere was best.

Because they both agreed to have a small guest list, they narrowed down guests to about fifty people. Only close family and friends were invited; and because they both had small families, that number worked out perfectly. The next few weeks were spent doing cake tastings, selecting the reception menu, finalizing the guest list based on RSVPs, securing a photographer and taking care of their wardrobes.

Many times during the wedding planning, Caleb wanted to stop and tell Raegan about Nicholas, but he was certain that she would want to put a hold on the wedding. She had gone through so much over the last couple of months that she was too fragile to deal with the situation rationally, so he continued to withhold Nicholas' existence. He convinced himself that he needed more time and so did she. Besides, he'd put off returning to Atlanta to get the results since they started the wedding planning. Somehow not having the official results gave him yet another excuse to withhold the information.

∞

Once again Raegan found herself on the arm of her father waiting to walk down the aisle to marry the man she'd always wanted to spend the rest of her life with. She stood taking in the scenery—from the beautiful white chairs adorned with white lilies on either side of the aisle to her grinning groom waiting to take her hand in marriage.

"Are you sure you're ready for this, baby girl?" Her father leaned over and whispered, reminding her of the last time he walked her down the aisle to a waiting groom.

"I've never been so sure of anything," she assured her father, smiled and kissed him on the cheek.

Etta James' *At Last* began to play through the speakers, signaling that it was time for her to join her groom at the staged altar, which was an arch adorned with gardenias. Raegan glided toward Caleb on the arm of her father, oblivious to the smiling faces of friends and family and camera phones held up from all directions.

She wanted to remember every part of that moment—the joy in Caleb's face and the mouthing of "you look beautiful." A black tuxedo with a mint green cummerbund and tie covered his muscular, six-foot frame. His brown eyes glistened and his smile reminded her of the day she first met him. He waited for her outside of their business calculus class to ask if she would tutor him. Both he and she knew that he didn't need her help, but that was the only way he knew to ask her out, and she had a crush on him so she accepted.

She held his gaze and mouthed back, "I love you," as tears escaped her eyes. The time had finally come for her to marry *the one God kept for her until it was time*. The words in Maurette Brown Clark's song could not have rung truer in that moment.

The ring bearer whispered to Caleb, "She looks like an angel."

"I know. God sent her to me," Caleb agreed, and that is what he believed. He loved her more than he had ever loved any woman, and he was thankful that she'd accepted his proposal and agreed to spend the rest of her life loving him.

As Raegan neared the altar, Caleb inhaled slowly and deeply and took in her beauty. He was always enthralled with the way her curls flowed loosely over her back. Her skin looked even more silky than usual as it sparkled with what appeared to be some kind of body glitter. Her fairytale wedding dress made her look as if she was a princess—white, sequined and strapless with a sweetheart neckline, lace-up back, beaded trim, along with a three-foot train, decorated with a water lily pattern. The sunlight highlighted the crystal beading, rhinestones and sequins perfectly. Her silver pumps added another two inches to her height and the wedding veil was pinned to her hair with a pearl clip.

Raegan's father placed her hand into Caleb's, patted his back, kissed Raegan's cheek once more and added, "Welcome to the family, son." Caleb and Raegan then walked hand in hand and stood in front of the preacher to begin the ceremony.

As the ceremony progressed, Raegan and Caleb stood hand in hand, face to face, smiling and whispering "I love you."

When it came time to say their vows, Caleb went first. They had prepared their own vows. Caleb's heart was so full of joy that his vows sounded more like a speech.

"Raegan Camille Sanders . . . It was as if the Lord smiled down on me the day I met you. I'm forever thankful for the day you agreed to tutor me," he said, chuckling softly. "A man who finds a wife finds a good thing and finds favor with the Lord. You, babe, are my favor. I love you with all of my heart and I vow to do my best to show you that by waking up each day, dying to myself and living for us. I vow to keep you first and be attentive to your needs as your husband. I vow to put your needs before mine and do all that I can to make sure that you are well taken care of in every area of your life when it is in my power to do so. I chose you the moment I laid eyes on you, and today I want to thank you for choosing me too. Some days you may regret that choice but I pray that you are happy about it more times than not." He smiled and wiped away a lone tear sliding down her cheek before finishing with, "I love you Cami, and each day the good Lord allows me to live, I will show you that. . . . By the way, you look gorgeous today."

"My sweet Caleb," Raegan began, her throat hurting from choking back tears. She exhaled deeply to regain her composure before she continued. "You're welcome." She giggled nervously while he and the guests laughed. She bit her bottom lip in an attempt to hold back the tears again. She never would have thought she'd be so emotional.

"Your love inspires me to be a better woman and I am so happy that I get to be that better woman by your side. You have such a forgiving heart and I'm forever thankful to God for that. I vow to love you even when I don't feel like it, to honor you, respect you, and treat you like the king that you are. For so long, I thought this day would never come, but God has been faithful to me, even when I have been unfaithful. He has been true to His Word by giving me the desires of my heart. And my desire has been you . . . always has. Thank you for loving me even when I didn't want it. From this point forward, I promise to love you, cherish you and give you as many babies as you want," she said as the crowd burst into laughter and whistles. "Within reason of course. So today, I promise to be a wife pleasing to both God and you. I love you, Caleb."

Now it was Raegan's turn to wipe the dampness away from Caleb's eyes. The ceremony continued with the exchanging of the rings and the consumption of holy communion together for the first time as husband and wife. The pastor prayed for them, blessed their union and made the official announcement to the guests.

"For the first time in eternity, I now present to you, Mr. and Mrs. Caleb McKinney."

Both husband and wife walked down the aisle to pose for pictures and greet their guests before moving under the tent to enjoy the reception activities. Raegan was truly happy for the first time in a while. Her rainbow after the storm. She was now married to the man who had stolen her heart so long ago; and although she regretted losing her baby, she was also happy she wasn't carrying a child conceived out of wedlock with another man.

Caleb experienced happiness mixed with guilt. He hadn't planned on withholding the information regarding Nicholas' existence from Raegan for this long. He couldn't believe he married her before ever telling her the truth. He had to come up with a plan quickly before she thought him a liar for everything he'd just promised her in his vows.

The DJ introduced Raegan and Caleb once more when they entered the tent and went straight into their first dance to John

Legend's *All of Me*. Caleb sang throughout the entire song as he danced and kissed his bride repeatedly.

The guests smiled and adored the couple as they enjoyed their first hour together as husband and wife. After their first dance, Raegan danced with her father and Caleb with his mother. Without wasting any time, she tossed the bouquet to her single friends and Michelle caught the bouquet. Caleb teasingly removed the garter from Raegan's thigh and tossed it to his single friends while Michael Jackson's *The Way You Make Me Feel* played. Most of his single friends didn't want to be in that number for fear their dates would be looking to get married next.

After toasts by the maid of honor and best man, more dinner and dancing, the guests were starting to leave as it was getting late and the temperature was starting to drop. Caleb and Raegan bid their guests good-bye and Caleb scooped Raegan off her feet and carried her to the limousine.

When they arrived home, Caleb carried her into the house and upstairs to their bedroom. It was their time. The moment had finally arrived when they could give themselves to each other without the concern of breaking celibacy vows, pregnancy outside of marriage or anything else that would cause them to have reservations.

"Mrs. McKinney, you look beautiful tonight," he said, untying her gown and planting warm gentle kisses along her neck and shoulders. It felt so good to be able to kiss his wife and fully give himself to her—mind, body and soul.

"I love you," she whispered in between her elevated breaths. "Always have and always will." Caleb paused for a moment, considering her admission as he thought about Nicholas, but now surely wasn't the time for that conversation.

"No matter what?" he asked as he lifted her by the hips, walked over, and placed her on their new bed. This would be the first time that either of them slept on it. It was delivered a few days ago but he wanted the first time he lay on it to be with her.

"No matter what," she assured him, resting her head on the pillow and pulling him toward her for another kiss. And he did just that, expressing his love to her by covering her body with kisses, warming every part of her, something he planned to do for the rest of his life.

# CHAPTER 27

"I have to go to Atlanta for work again, babe. I tried to get out of it, but the board wants me to be present to give my update this quarter," Caleb said, kissing her on the back of her neck.

Raegan rolled over to face him, her smile fading at the thought of him leaving again when they'd only been married for six weeks.

"When do you go? How long will you be gone? Do they not know that you recently got married?" She sighed and kissed his lips. "Do you want me to come with you? I don't mind taking a few days off work. My boss has been pretty understanding of the fact that I'm newly married. I don't know how long it will last, though."

"No," he said abruptly. He was planning to see Nicholas while he was there. In fact, the trip was actually about him. He would be getting the results of the paternity test; he had put it off far too long already. That would help him choose how to move forward. If the results were a match, he promised himself that he would tell her when he returned.

"Excuse me then," she said, rolling out of his embrace.

"Wait, where are you going? Even though the honeymoon is over, there is no reason why we can't use this Saturday morning as an opportunity to do honeymoon type stuff," he said, brushing her lips with a kiss as he pulled her back into his arms. He hadn't meant for his response to come off rude or as if he didn't want her to come along; she just couldn't come this time. That would be a fight waiting to happen. Their first fight as newlyweds.

Raegan couldn't resist being in his arms once more. She chose not to argue with him about going to Atlanta. She had plenty of work to catch up on and could probably spend some time writing thank-you notes.

"So when do you have to leave?"

"Next week. I'll only be gone a couple of days. Leaving Monday morning and back Wednesday morning. Just enough time for you to miss me and have some of that tender lovin' waiting for me when I come home," he answered between planting kisses over her body.

"Oh yeah," she squealed, reveling in his love once more.

∞

Caleb arrived in Atlanta and made his return trip to the hospital to pick up his test results his priority. He had no plans on going to work that day, because the meeting he mentioned to his wife wasn't until the next day. He needed time to process whatever the results were and didn't want to have it weighing heavily on his mind while trying to do his job, especially since his life was potentially about to change forever.

After picking up his results, Caleb went back to his car with the intent of opening the letter when he arrived at his hotel. He sat behind the steering wheel wondering what the results were. He'd been waiting for a couple of months now, and having this thing hanging over his head and in between him and his wife was driving him crazy. The waiting had become unbearable, so he ripped one end of the envelope and pulled the letter out and slowly opened it, not knowing how to prepare himself for this moment.

As he read the results, tears began to fill his eyes. He knew it! Why would Natalie do this to him? He had only partly thought about how he would handle things based on the results. He just knew that he had to tell Raegan either way, but first he needed to see Natalie. She would have to drop everything she was doing to address this today.

Caleb called Natalie and summoned her to the bistro down the street from the hotel to discuss Nicholas' paternity. After making arrangements to meet her in a couple of hours, he tossed the letter on top of his briefcase that sat in the passenger seat. After all of this time, he couldn't believe that he had a son and that Natalie had kept his son away from him.

There was no issue as to whether or not he would be in Nicholas' life; that was a given. His concern was how to break the news to his wife. He figured she'd be upset but she'd eventually get over it; he just didn't know exactly *how* she would take the news. She'd recently been deceived and betrayed, and the last thing he wanted was for her to feel like he was also doing that to her. He needed to talk to her.

Caleb called Raegan on the way to his hotel to let her know that he made it safely and was preparing for work. He took pleasure in hearing the sweetness of her voice because things would certainly change after he made it home and shared the news with her.

"I miss you beautiful. You know I'll always love you, right?"

"I'm pretty certain of it. I miss you too. I wish I could have come with you. It is way too early in our marriage for us to be spending nights apart. I've grown so used to you sleeping next to me already; how am I going to sleep tonight?" she purred, her voice melting his heart.

Caleb hoped she remembered those words after she found out about Nicholas. He knew her all too well and he was positive she would want to bolt. *But we're married now,* he thought.

"Don't worry Cami . . . if I have anything to do with it, our nights apart will be few and far between after this trip. I knew you had things to catch up on and didn't want you to waste your personal time to come out here for this. Save it for a real vacation. Or at least a staycation when we can both be free of work."

"Hmmm . . . staycation? I like the sound of that. Maybe we'll have to do that sooner than later."

"That can certainly be arranged. Anything for you, beautiful."

"I'm going to hold you to that, too. I love you, husband, but I have a meeting soon. Let me make sure I have everything ready for that and I'll talk with you later, okay?" She blew kisses into the phone.

"Okay, I'll call you around lunch time," he said. They shared more sentiments of loving and missing each other before ending the call.

Before he knew it, it was time for him to meet Natalie at the bistro. Caleb sat outside on the patio while waiting for her to arrive. He texted his wife a couple of times and placed the phone in his pocket when Natalie arrived.

Since Raegan's number was the last number called and texted, his phone dialed her while in his pocket. Raegan said hello a few times and was about to hang up because she assumed that he must have called her by mistake. But hearing the voice of another woman and Caleb mention the words "my son" gave her pause.

# CHAPTER 28

"Why did you wait nearly two years to tell me about my son?" Caleb asked Natalie after the quick exchange of pleasantries. It was after his relationship with her that he made a choice to become celibate. It wasn't that he slept with many women, but he was on a path to become the man that he believed God wanted him to be. And he knew he couldn't do that if he didn't surrender everything to God—including his fleshly desires.

He and Natalie split because they were on two totally different paths. Natalie attended church services weekly but had no desire to change her lifestyle beyond that, and since he wanted to settle down soon, he couldn't continue in a relationship with someone who didn't share the same values as he did. But now they shared a child.

"I wasn't planning to keep him from you; I actually didn't know whether or not he was yours, but the older he gets, the more he starts to look like you. And I know you didn't approve of my lifestyle so—"

"Excuse me? That is no reason to keep this kind of information from me. I should have known about him the moment you found out you were pregnant, Natalie!" Caleb banged his hand on the table in frustration.

"We were always so careful, so I was sure that he wasn't yours. Give me a little credit here. I came to you when I realized it. I didn't completely leave you out in the cold."

Caleb let out a quick sigh and shook his head.

"I suppose you want a thank you?" There was no mistaking the disgust in his voice that matched the scowl on his face.

"Whatever Caleb. How do you want to handle this?" Natalie's anxiety was evident with her fidgeting in her seat. "There is no need for us to run around in circles discussing why I didn't tell you. All that matters now is that you know. What are you going to do about it? Keep flying out here every month to take him to the park?" Natalie snapped back, clearly irritable. She'd been overwhelmed and suffering from a lack of sleep for the last year, ever since Nicholas' birth. Even though Nicholas was sleeping most of the night, her feelings of depression had yet to cease.

Raegan sat in her office with her door closed, phone on mute, listening to Caleb and Natalie's conversation, at least what she could make out of it. *Caleb has a child.* Her heart sank. Here she was recently married and her husband had a child that she knew nothing about. She wondered how long he had known about the child. *Apparently long enough to make frequent trips to Atlanta to see him and not tell me about it.*

He knew about his son before the wedding and he kept it from her. She wanted to scream but she couldn't do that at work so she sobbed, drowning out the office sounds of copiers and ringing telephones outside of her door. Familiar feelings washed over her. Betrayal. Thoughts of why she left him in college and Rico's deceit flooded her mind. What was she supposed to do with this information? Wait on him to come clean?

She didn't want to listen anymore, but it seemed as if this would be the only way she would get the truth, so she dabbed her eyes, blew her nose and put the phone back to her ear.

"No, we have to make better arrangements than that. Obviously this is going to be difficult since I've moved to Texas, but we'll have to work something out. We can discuss it more over the next few weeks. In the meantime, I need to discuss this with my wife."

"I noticed the symbol of love wrapped around your finger," she said, pointing to his wedding band. "So what does discussing it with your wife mean? Does she not know about Nicholas at all?"

Caleb squinted in frustration. He knew that Natalie was being messy, although she was right about his end of the situation.

"We just have to work out our schedules in order for Nicholas to spend time with us and get to know us. We'll both be a part of his life; I hope you understand that," he said. *I hope Cami understands that too,* he thought to himself.

"I have no problem with that, but I'd like to meet her first. No offense to you, but I can't have my baby around just anybody. Bring her to Atlanta the next time you're here and we can all sit down and see what works best," suggested Natalie.

She actually made sense. Natalie was known to be irrational, but he actually thought that was a good idea and would definitely propose it to his wife during their discussion.

"Well, congratulations, you're a father now," Natalie said as she stood to leave. "Let me know when you plan to come back to town with the Mrs."

Caleb nodded and remained seated. He planned to sit there for a while to think. "I want to see Nicholas today. What time can you meet me?"

"Give me a couple of hours to run errands and I'll give you a call when I'm picking him up from daycare."

"Thanks, Natalie," Caleb said dryly. He prayed Raegan would understand when he explained things to her. She knew what it was like to have a child outside of their relationship; surely she'd be able to empathize and help him work out visitation arrangements so that they could get to know Nicholas better.

When Raegan realized the meeting was over, she hung up the phone. A son? She didn't know if she would tell Caleb she knew about it or wait for him to break the news to her. From the way he was talking, she figured he planned to tell her when he returned. It was definitely not a discussion to be held over the phone, but she didn't want to wait until he came back.

Her thoughts were soon interrupted by his call. She just let the phone ring. She couldn't answer it. She didn't press ignore because he would be able to hear it if she did, so she silenced the ringer. She had so many things to consider. She wasn't ready to be a mother to someone else's child, especially when she wanted to birth her own. *But he was prepared to stay with you and raise another man's baby,* her conscience reminded her. That was true, but she wasn't ready for this. She was hurting not only because he kept it from her, but also because he had with someone else what she wanted with him.

# CHAPTER 29

Joshua's concern over their financial issues was becoming a thing of the past as his thoughts were now filled with the idea of starting a family—a topic that he brought up every day in hopes that he could convince Tammy that they should get started sooner than later. Tammy wanted to start a family, too, but thoughts of her career being put on hold and Joshua's heart condition being hereditary gave her pause. She'd given him hope that she was ready but had secretly started taking birth control pills. It seemed that was her only choice until she could come to terms with everything and keep him happy at the thought that they were trying to conceive.

She wasn't planning on taking the birth control for too long, only long enough to make sure that he fully recovered, her career wouldn't be in jeopardy and she gathered more information about the effects his condition could have on their children.

Joshua and Tammy's renewal ceremony was perfect and stress free, which they both attributed to them working out their differences regarding finances. They were both on cloud nine as they celebrated their reunion with their guests at the Bell Tower on 34th. "You know I love you, right?" he whispered to her in between greeting guests and posing for photos, as they stood in the center of the shiny marble-tiled floor under chandelier lighting. Tammy wore a floor length, one shoulder, satin gown that sported a split up to her knee on both sides, and her shoulder length curls were dazzled with a diamond-laced tiara that sparkled in the chandelier lighting. She looked the part of a famous NBA player's wife.

"Yes. And I love you," she said, lifting her head so that he could kiss her.

"Oooh, don't you two look cute!" Michelle exclaimed, interrupting the happy couple. She was glad to see her friend finally getting her shot of happiness. She stood next to them and handed her phone to another guest to snap a photo of her with the couple.

"Thank you!" they said in unison as Tammy hugged her friend. Joshua hugged Michelle and then excused himself to talk with a few of his friends while Tammy and Michelle chatted.

"I'm so happy for you. How are you doing these days? I know you've had your hands full lately with work, caring for Josh, and planning this shindig, which is awesome by the way," Michelle complimented, popping a half-bitten strawberry into her mouth.

"I'm great," Tammy sang and smiled. After praying and deciding to compromise on the finance issue, she felt an unspeakable amount of peace. But there was still the baby issue.

They walked arm in arm across the room, chatting in between Tammy stopping and speaking to her guests and posing for more photos. Michelle then mentioned that she had noticed Raegan seemed distant and brushed off her concern when Michelle brought it up to her. Michelle wondered if Tammy had noticed it too.

Michelle was pretty excited when she saw Raegan and embraced her warmly, but in return, Raegan gave her a half-hearted, one-arm hug and pasted smile. Michelle knew something was bothering her but Raegan dismissed Michelle's questions as if she was imagining it.

"Hey, I think I just heard my name." Raegan walked up to Tammy and Michelle and smiled. She hugged them for a second time that night, this time with more feeling. She knew them well enough to know that they probably suspected something was wrong with her, even though she'd been trying hard to hide her funky mood. She was still waiting on her husband to tell her about Nicholas.

"Hey you! How is married life treating you?" Tammy asked, trying to feel her out to see if the issue Michelle mentioned involved her new husband.

"Everything is fine," she lied, glancing over to Caleb and giving him a sly smile. She waved him over to say hello to her friends. He joined the ladies, exchanged pleasantries and returned to Joshua and the other guys.

Tammy watched them closely. She knew it wasn't her business, but something obviously was going on between them. Raegan was generally a private person and she knew that she would tell them when she was ready, so she didn't probe too much.

"So how are things with Caleb's transition here?" Tammy asked, eyeing Raegan carefully.

"Oh, things are good. He likes the new position and seems to be enjoying Houston quite well. But, he seems to have a few things in Atlanta to keep him going back, and it doesn't seem like that will end any time soon," Raegan complained a little.

Tammy didn't miss the tone in which Raegan spoke and figured that must be the sore spot. However, she left it alone and switched the subject to something less tense.

As Caleb returned to the guys, he couldn't help but feel like Raegan knew everything. *That can't be true,* he thought. There was no way she could have known. Not that he was being sneaky, but he had been sure to cover his tracks.

∞

Caleb took a break from the reception to pray. He went to his car and had a good old-fashioned talk with the Lord.

"Heavenly Father, you know the situation that I'm in. You know my heart, and my intention was never to deceive my wife. I pray that You help her to see the same. So, I come seeking You and asking that You provide the right time and opportunity for me to share the news about Nicholas with her. I ask that You give her a welcoming and understanding heart so that we may work through this together. I appreciate You bringing her back into my life and I can't lose her now. I believe that You're going to bless us with a long, happy and fulfilling marriage. I want to be the husband that Your Word says I should be, loving my wife as myself. And I believe by faith that our dependence on Your love for us and our love for one another will see us through."

Caleb continued, "Your Word does say that love is patient, love is kind. It does not envy, it does not boast, it is not proud. It does not dishonor others, it is not self-seeking, it is not easily angered, it keeps no record of wrongs. Love does not delight in evil but rejoices with the truth. It always protects, always trusts, always hopes, always perseveres. Love never fails. So I thank You for Your Word, Lord, and ask that You show me favor in this. In Jesus' name, Amen."

Caleb lifted his head in enough time to see Raegan walking toward the car. He couldn't help but think that Raegan knew about Nicholas, because she had been distant ever since he returned from Atlanta. It was as if she was waiting on him to confess, providing an opportunity at every turn, but perhaps that was the guilt making him feel that way. Regardless of that, he was going to tell her before going to bed tonight. He vowed not to allow another day pass before he told her the truth. He loved her too much to keep it from her; he just prayed that she loved him enough to understand.

"Hey," she said, tapping the window. When he rolled it down, she continued, "I've been looking for you. Is this where you've been all this time?"

"Yes, I didn't think I'd be gone for too long; I just needed to step away and clear my head for a minute."

"Is it clear now?" she asked, wondering if he was about to tell her the truth.

"Something like that." He stepped out of the car and fidgeted with his keys for a moment. "Are you ready to leave, or would you like to stay a while longer?"

"I think I've had enough socializing for tonight. We can leave as soon as you're ready."

Raegan and Caleb returned to the party to say goodnight to their friends and extend their well wishes. When Raegan hugged Tammy one final time, Tammy whispered into her ear, "Whatever it is, it will be just fine. I know it will. If nothing else, God has your back and so do your friends," Tammy said, winking as she pulled out of her embrace.

Raegan looked confused for a moment but thanked Tammy and hugged Joshua before leaving. She and Caleb walked back to the car, hand in hand, in silence. She wondered what he was doing in the car before she showed up. Was he on the phone with the woman she heard him speaking with? Was he talking to this son he had not mentioned to her? The entire situation was starting to bother her; it just didn't sit well. And the longer Caleb waited to talk to her about it, the more she felt like he was trying to hide something from her. This was important. *Why would he keep something like this a secret? How long has he known?*

Caleb opened the passenger door and helped her into the car. Once she was safely inside, he closed the door and went around to the driver's side. *Please Lord, I need You,* he prayed silently.

The ride home was mostly silent. Raegan was waiting for him to speak and he was trying to find the right words so that she would know that he never intended to hurt or deceive her. When they arrived home, they changed into more comfortable clothing. Raegan wore a pair of sweats while Caleb wore a pair of faded blue jeans and a white T-shirt.

"Cami, sweetheart, we need to talk," he began, taking both of her hands into his as they sat on the sofa.

"Yeah, I think it's about time we do . . ."

# CHAPTER 30

Caleb sat for a moment, looking into Raegan's eyes and trying to read her mood. She'd been silent for the past few days, even tonight at Tammy and Joshua's party. It was as if something had changed when he returned from his trip.

"I've always loved you and nothing will ever change that." Caleb massaged her hands as he spoke. Raegan remained still and silent. "Cami, getting a second chance with you has been the best thing that's happened to me in a really long time. I hope you know that." She still remained expressionless, waiting for him to tell her the whole truth. Seeing as though she wasn't giving him any reassurance, he took a deep breath and continued.

He told her about Natalie and his relationship with her before choosing to become celibate. He and Natalie were engaged in a sexual relationship for about a year when he decided that he no longer wanted to be involved with her. She didn't desire to be a woman who loved, submitted to, or respected a man in the way that God's Word demonstrates. In fact, she didn't want to do anything more than attend church on Sundays. She wasn't looking to change or to live a life pleasing to God. And for him, that was a deal breaker. He didn't want to marry anyone like her. In fact, his heart still belonged to Raegan.

At that point, Raegan pulled her hands away from his, folded her legs Indian style, got comfortable and waited for him to tell her what she needed to hear. She still said nothing. At that point, he was certain she knew; he just wasn't sure how.

"Fast forward nearly two years later after she and I called it quits; she showed up at my house in Atlanta when I returned for the closing. She stood in my doorway holding a little boy who looked just like I did as a child."

"That was before our wedding, Caleb. You didn't think it was important enough to tell me before we said 'I do'?" Raegan jumped off the couch and folded her arms across her chest. She was noticeably breathing heavier and her eyes were beginning to water from the hurt and betrayal she'd been feeling.

"I didn't want to lose you again," he continued. He rubbed the back of his neck as if it pained him to say that. She'd left him before and he didn't want that to happen again. He would much rather risk her being upset with him now than to have told her sooner only to watch her disappear for the next ten years.

"How do you know what would have happened? You never even gave me a chance to listen, to understand, to be with you in all of this. Instead, you lied to me about why you needed to go to Atlanta. You claimed you were going for work, but now I'm sure it was to see this child. What's his name? Nicholas?"

"How do you know that?" His head popped up as he sat up straight and stared at her. Raegan paced and ranted about her feelings, explaining everything she knew and how she knew it.

"You must have butt dialed me when you met with Natalie the last time you were there. I heard everything. I just wondered how long it would take you to tell me. And you know what? It took you way too long. So tell me, what do you expect from me?" Raegan paused for a moment and stood in front of him, arms folded, grimacing.

"To continue loving me and to help me sort through this."

"Sort through what? The paternity test revealed he's your son, right? What is it you need to sort through? Sounds like you have it all figured out to me. I suppose you now want me to fly to

Atlanta with you to meet your old girlfriend so that she can give you her blessing to have your son around me? Me? Your wife?" Raegan seethed.

Caleb moved to where she was to stop her pacing and to get her to look him in the eyes. He needed her to know that he wasn't trying to hurt her. That was never his intention.

"Babe, look at me. I didn't want to hurt you. First, I needed to know that she was telling me the truth about Nicholas. That is why I kept it from you in the beginning. Then, when I found out the truth, I needed to find a way to tell you. I thought I was doing what was best for you and me. I love you, Cami. Can't you see that?"

"I thought I did, but apparently you don't love me enough to trust me with something as important as this. So what is your plan now?"

"To make sure that you and I are good. Are we?"

"I don't know. It's clear what you think of me. Although we said we would let the past go, you haven't. You still think I'm that naive twenty-year-old who left you without saying a word. Did you honestly think I would do that to you if you told me the truth before the wedding?" Raegan asked. She knew that she had hurt him before, but it pained her to think that he really hadn't gotten over that and was still holding it against her. She may not have gotten all the facts when she left him before, but she felt like she had more than enough information this time around to warrant her leaving if she chose to do so. *Where is the trust?* she wondered.

However, part of her knew that he was right. She probably would have called off the wedding and told him to go sort through everything with Natalie and Nicholas before he could marry her. But they would never know, because he chose not to let her in. That hurt.

"I didn't say that. I just needed to make sure that I had all of the facts and that you would understand when I told you everything. Please say you understand my choices. I promise that I was only thinking about us and our future," Caleb pleaded.

"I can't say that. I think I'm going to need some time to think about all of this. I'm going to bed," she said without another word to him. She trudged upstairs to pray, but instead found herself wanting time away to think. She had to get out of there, and luckily for her, she never completely unpacked all of her things when she moved in after the wedding.

Raegan wondered aloud as she tossed a few more items into a suitcase. What gave him the right to make the decision for her? He allowed this to go on way too long, leaving her with plenty of time to draw her own conclusions. And in her mind, it was all his fault for allowing this whole situation to fester. He should have told her he had a son as soon as he found out, she told herself the moment she overheard the conversation. She zipped the suitcase and lugged it down the stairs. She stood at the base and stared at him, her hand on the handle of the rolling leather bag. Caleb turned around to see her packed and ready to bolt—just like he thought she would. *Apparently God didn't answer my prayers,* he thought to himself as his eyes pleaded with her. He knew he would just be repeating himself, but he gave it another shot anyway.

"Cami, where are you going? I think we both know you need to be right here with me working this out. Now is not the time for you to leave." He walked over to her and placed his hand on the handle of the suitcase.

"Did you think of that, too, when you were keeping your little secret? Is that the way you're going to handle everything in our marriage?"

"Is this the way you're going to handle everything? Run every time I don't do things the way you think I should?" he retorted, rattling the handle on her suitcase.

"It doesn't feel good, does it?" she said over her shoulder as she walked out of the door, leaving him standing at the base of the stairs.

# CHAPTER 31

Tammy felt a twinge of guilt resurfacing as she lay spooning in bed with her husband. He was overjoyed at the thought that she would soon be carrying his first child. *I'm definitely being selfish now,* she thought. Everything that Joshua said to her during their argument about needing her pushed to the forefront of her thoughts. His emotions were raw when he said that to her and she vowed to always be there when he needed her from that point forward. She'd renewed her vows only to not fully give herself to him as she promised.

Her thoughts woke her up early that morning as she rationalized that taking birth control pills was the right thing to do for now. She snuggled closer to him as she thought about how she had missed out on waking up next to him every morning for more than ten years.

Joshua stirred, pulled her closer and kissed her shoulders.

"Good morning," he whispered, kissing her ear. "What do you want for breakfast?"

"You," she answered, rolled over and greeted him with a kiss. As they lay in bed, bodies intertwined, gazing into each other's eyes, Tammy's heart warmed at the joy in Joshua's eyes. He seemed so happy and peaceful.

Since they were starting fresh, she had to come clean. She couldn't lie in bed with him every night, giving him hope that they would soon have a child when she was doing everything in her power to prevent that from happening.

Tammy slid out of bed to shower while Joshua went into the kitchen to make pancakes, eggs and sausages. When Tammy finished her shower, she walked into the kitchen and stood in the doorway, watching Joshua, who had his back to her as he worked his way around the kitchen. She took a deep breath and walked up behind him, wrapping her arms around his waist.

"Babe, there's something I need to tell you."

"What's that?" He continued to cook with his back to her.

"I'm on the pill."

Joshua's body stiffened at the admission. He turned off the burners, peeled her fingers from his waist and turned around to look at her. "What do you mean?"

Tammy hunched her shoulders and walked away, sorting through her thoughts so that her explanation would sound as plausible to him as it did to her. She pulled out a leather seat from the marble breakfast table and sat down, wiping at an imaginary stain on the table.

"I'm scared. Scared of what may happen to you, the baby and my career. Too many uncertainties and what-ifs."

Joshua folded his arms across his chest and walked over to the table. He wanted to be angry with her for lying to him, but before reacting, he took a moment and put himself in her shoes. He understood how she could be worried with his health condition and the potential for their children to have it as well, but that was no reason to lie to him. He squatted in front of her and took her hands in his.

"Sweetheart, I understand but I'm pissed that you've been lying to me. Nothing in life is certain. Don't you know that?"

Tammy nodded. He was taking it a lot better than she thought he would. She said a silent prayer of thanks to God for giving Joshua a heart of gold and that she was a part of his treasure.

"We can't put our lives on hold because of fear. We gather all the information available to us, make the best choices we can and move forward. We have to put our faith in God and not live with the spirit of fear. We know that God is in control and He will see us through every circumstance."

Tammy nodded and Joshua continued, "We can always talk to the doctor about children, if that will make you feel better. And don't worry much about me, I've made a full recovery and I don't plan to check out anytime soon." He rubbed Tammy's chin and placed a lingering kiss on her lips.

Joshua pulled up a stool and sat in front of her as she expressed her concerns about their children having the heart condition. She didn't want to live with him not being around to help her raise their children nor have children who would suffer from the cardiomyopathy or any other heart condition.

Before Joshua had even brought up the subject, he'd done research and talked to his doctor. However, he knew Tammy needed to talk to the doctor as well to be comfortable with knowing that even if his condition was passed on to their children, it was manageable and they would likely be fine. They agreed to make an appointment to talk with the doctor so that she could toss the birth control pills to the trash.

"You know dear," Joshua said, making their plates, "we never really discussed where we would live. I know coming to Texas was part of my recovery, but now that I'm better, we can move to Boston. Have you given it any thought?"

"My career and friends are here, and I don't want to leave just yet. Besides, things are going so well for us here and you're likely going to get that analyst position with NBC. Isn't that what you want?" Tammy hoped.

"Honestly, I am open to living anywhere. I can fulfill this part of my dream in any part of the country. It's time to focus on what it is you want to do with your career. Are you sure you're happy here?"

"For now, yes." Tammy stood, leaving her place setting and walking over to sit on his lap. "I love you Mr. Archer. You know that, right?" she commented, caressing his face.

"Mrs. Archer, I love you with every fiber of my being," he echoed, giving her a toothy smile.

"Forgive me for keeping the pills a secret?"

"I may need some convincing."

Tammy linked her fingers behind his head and pulled him closer for another one of their long, lingering, passionate kisses. Joshua had already received a referral for a doctor in Houston and agreed that all would be forgiven if they went to see him as soon as possible. It was time to get the baby-making show on the road.

# CHAPTER 32

Raegan yanked the "For Sale" sign out of her yard when she arrived at her house. She wasn't quite sure why she did that, but the simple act empowered her and made her feel a little better. She tossed it to the side in her garage and went inside. She was grateful that her home hadn't sold, because she now had a place of refuge. She needed time to think about everything.

"How am I supposed to take the news that my husband has a son and I just found out that I'm pregnant? This was supposed to be our moment, and yet, here we are again with something, well *someone,* in the middle of it!" Raegan mulled over her situation as she walked through her home, inspecting it to make sure that all was well.

She needed to talk with someone, but she didn't want to discuss her marital problems with anyone else. She couldn't call her mom, because she knew her mom would tell her to go home to her husband and to keep her out of it. That wouldn't be of any help to her.

She couldn't call her best friend, Kensi, because Kensi would remind her that Caleb was still marrying her even when she was pregnant with Rico's child. Kensi would tell her that she was wrong and that she had no right not to stand by him while he was going through this, when he stood by her when she went through her difficult time. But this was completely different in Raegan's eyes and Kensi wouldn't see it that way.

Raegan had to face it. No one would understand her decision to *take a break*. She knew it was unrealistic and that there were no breaks in marriage, but that was what she felt like she needed right now. She cried every time she thought of Caleb keeping the knowledge of Nicholas away from her. She even caught an attitude with random strangers, like the server at Sonic who didn't remember she said no whipped cream on her caramel sundae. Maybe it was the hormones making her feel that way, but either way, she was wearing her feelings on her sleeves. She needed to sleep on it, so she decided to deal with it in the morning as she snuggled under the sheets in her old bed.

∞

"What are you doing here?" Raegan's mom asked her. After tossing and turning most of the night, Raegan came up with the idea that she would take an impromptu trip to visit her parents' home in Florida. She figured paying a visit to her family would help her take her mind off things long enough so that she could think rationally. She purchased an expensive, last minute plane ticket and headed for Houston Hobby Airport. The only person who knew about the trip was Kensi, although Raegan didn't reveal why she was taking the trip or that she was taking it without her newly wedded husband. She'd learned that it was best to tell at least one person where you were going in case of an accident.

"I just thought I would surprise you." Raegan lied through her teeth and her mom knew it.

It didn't slip past her mom that Caleb was not standing at her daughter's side in her doorway. She knew that Raegan could be extreme, and after sizing her up, she assumed that Raegan was likely running from something. For some strange reason, she always seemed to run away when it came to Caleb. Raegan couldn't wait to skip town and move to Texas upon graduation from college in an attempt to get away from her issues with Caleb. She was always an excellent student and she'd had several co-ops and volunteer opportunities while in school, so she could have easily started her career in Florida. But Raegan needed something different, or at least that is what she told her mom. She didn't fool her mom one bit then, and she wasn't fooling her now.

Her mom blocked her entrance into the house, placing both hands on either side of the door frame.

"So you aren't going to let me in? Aren't you happy to see your only daughter?" Raegan said through a fake smile.

"That depends on why she's here," her mom retorted, standing with her head cocked to one side, curiously eyeing her daughter.

"What do you mean? I told you that I came to surprise you," said Raegan, feigning her innocence.

"That's what you told me, but you and I both know that isn't the truth. What are you running from this time?" her mom questioned. She never really got into Raegan's business when she left Damian at the altar. She didn't push the issue and figured that Raegan would someday tell her the truth. Since she was Raegan's mother, she knew her well and she was almost certain it had everything to do with the man who wasn't standing there with her now.

"I'm not running from anything . . . Dad!" Raegan yelled over her mom's shoulder.

"Oh, he's not here, dear," her mom said and smiled mischievously. "Where is *your* husband?"

Raegan rolled her eyes and stood with her arms folded. Her mom shot her a glare that instantly removed the sassiness from Raegan's demeanor. *Why did I even come here for solace?* Raegan thought.

"Well, I don't think he's here either. Looks like it's just you and me," Raegan said, forcing a smile.

"Go home to your husband. I don't care what the issue is; you need to go home and work it out. The last place you should be right now is on my doorstep."

"What?"

"You heard me. Go home," her mom said over her shoulder as she walked away from the door. Raegan lugged her small carryon suitcase behind her, leaving it at the door to follow her mom through the house.

"I just need some time to think," Raegan whined.

"And you need to do that at home, not nearly one thousand miles away. You've only been married two months, if that, and you're already running away! Young people!" her mom continued tossing the words over her shoulder as Raegan followed behind her.

"I'm pregnant!" Raegan said, stopping her mom in her tracks. Her first grandchild! "But Caleb has a son already," Raegan blurted out before her mom could gush over the fact that she was about to become a grandma. Raegan took a seat at the dining room table, awaiting her mom's reaction.

As much as her mother wanted to stay out of the situation, now that there would be a grandchild involved, she figured that she would at least listen to whatever Raegan's issue seemed to be. She made them a pot of tea as Raegan shared what was bothering her. She recounted all of the details to her mom, including how she found out and how long it finally took Caleb to tell her, and then the moment he finally told her and the argument that followed. Raegan thought her mother would offer her some advice or at least take her side, but instead she just listened and sipped her tea.

When Raegan finished sharing her feelings about the situation, her mom repeated her earlier sentiments, "Baby, instead of sitting in my living room, you need to be sitting in your own living room discussing this with your husband. You made a vow for better or for worse, and it seems that in your mind this is closer to the 'for worse' end of the spectrum. But honey, I can assure you that there are far worse things than this." She rubbed Raegan's back as she took a sip of tea. "I can't tell you how to work it out; all I can say is that you have to. You took a vow for forever, and that can be a very long time depending on how long the good Lord allows you to walk this green earth."

Raegan sipped her own tea as she thought about her mother's advice. She knew she was right but wouldn't dare admit it right now.

They sat in silence while sipping the rest of their tea. When Raegan finished, she rubbed her stomach, and that seemed to light a spark in her mom's eyes.

"So, just how far along are you?" her mother asked, grinning from ear to ear.

"I don't know. I can't be that far along. I just tested positive a few days ago."

Her mom walked over and gave her a reassuring hug.

"Now take care of yourself and that baby," her mom cautioned. She wanted to ask how Caleb was taking the news, but she was fairly certain he wasn't aware of it.

The next morning, Raegan returned to Houston at the urging of her mother. She wasn't ready yet, but knew that nothing would get resolved between her and Caleb if she stayed away.

When Raegan left her mom's house, her mother called Caleb. "I'm sending your wife back home."

# CHAPTER 33

Caleb knew that he had messed up and that his wife was pretty upset with him, but he thought she'd just return to her old home a few miles away, not to her mom's house in Florida!

After hanging up with her mom, he placed his cell phone on the coffee table and sat with his hands clasped together, chin resting on them. What was he going to do with her? She definitely couldn't run away every single time they had a disagreement. Life didn't work that way, and it was about time she understood that.

Several hours later, when he was certain her plane had arrived and he hadn't heard anything from her, he figured that she went back to her old home. Caleb took a quick shower, dressed in jeans and a black featherweight sweater and dabbed on a little bit of Curve cologne—his wife's favorite scent. He grabbed his keys and headed straight for his car to do what any man in his position would do–find his wife.

When he pulled up to her driveway, it was just as he had suspected; she was there. The curtains were pulled back and the lights were on. He took the keys out of the ignition and opened the car door in one motion. *Lord, please help me with this woman You gave me,* he prayed silently, as he strode to the door with purpose. Everything about his demeanor said that he meant business. He stood at the door, feet apart, one hand in his pocket and the other resting on the doorbell, which he pushed several times before she answered.

Raegan peered through the peephole to see who was ringing her doorbell, as if she didn't already know. No one would be looking for her there except him. With all the thinking she'd done, she still hadn't quite thought of a way to resolve her issues with him or even what she wanted to say. It was inevitable; there was no way she would be able to hide there forever, so she opened the door. *May as well face the music now,* she thought.

He must have been worried about her, because he hadn't shaved in a couple of days, she concluded while standing in the doorway giving him a once-over. He was still as handsome as ever. As his new wife, what she really wanted to do was jump all over him and kiss him until her lips hurt, but she was mad. And to her, that was another way to prove her point, no bodily contact.

"Hello husband," she said through clenched teeth, hardly moving her lips, as she opened the door and stepped to the side so that he could come inside. With one eyebrow raised and one hand positioned on her hip, she was ready for battle.

Everything about her stance said that she was prepared for combat and so was he; but when their eyes locked, he silently called a truce. Without saying a word or giving his wife enough time to protest, he pulled her into his arms and kissed her passionately, just the way newlyweds should be kissing right about now. He was upset at her behavior and the way she was treating him, but that did not get in the way of him missing her and wanting her in his arms. For a moment, Raegan forgot her feelings about the secret he'd kept from her and everything that had transpired over the past few days and reciprocated the kiss.

Before long, they found themselves loving each other completely. No words had been spoken about their ensuing conflict, only reconnecting in mind, body and soul.

"I apologize for handling things the way I did. I love you, Cami," Caleb said after he'd done his very best to prove that through their lovemaking. She now lay cuddled upon his chest listening to his heart beat as it slowly went back to its resting state.

"I love you, too," she whispered. She never moved to look at him. She rubbed her hand across his chest as she thought about why she was upset with him in the first place. She didn't want the situation to get any worse than it was, but she wanted him to know how deeply he'd hurt her.

"We cannot resolve our problems if you run away every time we get into a disagreement." He pulled her closer to him. If he could have pulled her inside of himself, he would have. That is how much she was a part of him, and he wanted her to understand that.

Raegan remained silent. She agreed with him. She knew she couldn't run away, but at the time, it felt like the most logical thing for her to do. She didn't want to be in the same house with him. She felt betrayed. Again. She wasn't the same twenty-year-old who left him before, but she had surely acted like it and for that, she was wrong. She had the tendency to be dramatic and that seemed to be the only thing that would help him see how he'd made her feel. He needed to remember what life would be like without her; at least that's what she'd told herself.

"So how do you propose we handle this?" She sat up in bed and turned to face him, with her feet curled under her. She pulled the sheets up to her chest, wrapping them under her arms as she made herself comfortable.

"In a way that is best for everyone involved. Does it bother you that I have a son, or does it bother you that I waited to tell you?" he asked, seeking to see things the way she perceived them. He had been dreading her feelings about the issue. He wanted her to be happy about Nicholas' being in their lives. He wanted her to want to get to know the little boy, just as he did.

Raegan thought carefully. He would likely not understand her point of view. She didn't want him to have a child with another woman. She had nothing against the little boy, but if she were to be honest, it bothered her. She wasn't sure to what extent it bothered her, but it just didn't sit well with her. She wanted to be the one to carry his children, not anyone else. Although she was carrying one at the moment, it just wasn't the same.

She wanted to say that she wished to be the only one to share that with him, but he could always remind her of the baby Rico fathered with her. He could also bring up the fact that he didn't run when he found out she was pregnant and there was a possibility that he wasn't the father—or even when he knew that he was not. He stayed and chose to be with her anyway. He would even raise the child as his own. So why did she have such a problem with this situation?

"I don't know." Caleb tilted his head to encourage her to continue. He needed more than the brief response that she'd given.

"What does that mean? Considering everything that we've gone through together, including me standing beside you with all of your Rico drama, I think I deserve a better answer than that." He wanted to bring up the fact that he didn't act the way she was acting when he found out about her baby, but he knew that was still a sore spot with her and he didn't want to reopen that wound. He believed that she was still hurt about losing the baby.

"I just . . . ," she sighed. "I just thought after I lost the baby that the next time there was a baby between the two of us that it would be created by us. That's all. I know that you can't do anything about it now, but it still hurts my feelings a little that my husband has a child with someone else. One that he kept from me for God knows how long." There, she said it. She was honest enough, she thought. She wasn't sure if now was the right time to bring up the fact that she was pregnant, because she figured he would somehow use that in his argument.

"Babe, I don't know how to explain it, but Nicholas has nothing to do with that. We can create as many babies as you want together. But I do want to be in his life. No son should have to grow up without his father."

"I can agree with that." Oddly enough, she agreed with him even though she asked Rico to sign over his parental rights. *But this is different,* she thought. *Caleb was willing to treat the child as his own so the baby wouldn't have grown up without a father.* She could only take this one day at a time, because she honestly didn't know what else to do. What she did know was that she didn't want to lose her husband over her issues with him having a child from a prior relationship. Raegan repositioned herself to sit on his lap and sealed their agreement with a kiss. She then caressed his cheeks and kissed both of his eyelids. His eyes were so intense and focused as he presented his point that she couldn't help herself. Her heart was bursting with joy at his desire to be the man he needed to be in her life and in his son's.

# CHAPTER 34

For what seemed like the hundredth time since tossing her birth control pills, Tammy was taking another pregnancy test as Joshua stood outside of the bathroom door with a timer, waiting for the result.

At first, Tammy did not leave the restroom, but at the sound of the timer, she opened the door and asked her husband to look at the digital results. She did not want to see another *not pregnant* reading on the slender white stick. She extended the stick toward him and turned her head.

He remained silent for a few seconds too long and she assumed that it must have been negative again. She turned her head slightly to take a peek at his face and noticed a huge grin.

"Does that mean . . . "

"Yes! A little ball player!" In all of his excitement, he pulled her close to him, lifting her off her feet, and kissed her lips and then her belly.

"Thank you Lord!" Tammy squealed, but then she remembered Joshua's heart condition. They had already met with his doctor and her obstetrician to discuss the risks but it was different now; the pregnancy test was positive. Everything the doctors told them about cardiomyopathy and genetics suddenly rushed to the forefront of her mind. Even if the baby did have the heart condition, there was only a slim chance of it becoming serious. She silently prayed for the baby and that Joshua would be around to see the baby grow up.

"Looks like we finally did it. I think that is the most work I've put in since being off the court," he said and laughed.

"Oh and it is much appreciated." She smiled and kissed him, taking the stick away from him and tossing it to the trash.

"First things first. We have to get you to the doctor and make sure that everything is okay."

∞

Joshua saw to it that Tammy received care from the best doctor in the city, Dr. Lena Spencer. He knew there was a chance that the baby could have some sort of heart condition because his heart condition, cardiomyopathy, could be genetic. He figured that if they received the best care early on, the doctors could quickly identify any issues and monitor the baby's heart, put Tammy on bedrest or whatever it took to ensure they had a healthy baby.

The couple sat in Dr. Spencer's waiting room, patiently waiting to be seen. Dr. Spencer was a highly sought after ob/gyn because of her track record with taking care of her patients and excellent bedside manners. Because she was the best, she hardly had time in her schedule for new patients, but with Joshua's status and money, there was always a way around the red tape.

Joshua prayed silently, holding Tammy's hand. All of the things that could be wrong with the baby ran through his mind. Couple that with his recent health scare. He silently prayed that God would have mercy on them and allow them to have a healthy baby and allow him the opportunity to help Tammy raise the baby.

"Hey, are you all right?" Tammy asked. She figured that some of her anxiety must have been rubbing off on him because his hands felt extremely warm considering the low temperature of the room.

"I'm good," he said with a small wince.

"Are you sure?"

Her probing was interrupted by the nurse calling them back to see the doctor. Once Tammy had given all of her samples and the nurse left them alone, Tammy asked Joshua to pray for them. He agreed, continuing the silent prayer that he was in the middle of just moments ago. He prayed for his family, for their strength, and for each of them individually. He felt the need to be specific about what He needed God to do in their lives, supporting his requests with Scripture. As Joshua ended the prayer with Amen, the doctor walked in to perform an ultrasound and check the baby's heartbeat. She was aware of Joshua's medical condition based on the medical forms that Tammy filled out and wanted to get to it right away.

While performing the ultrasound, the doctor confirmed that Tammy was about seven weeks pregnant. She watched the monitor and listened closely to the heartbeat for several minutes. She noticed a few skips in the baby's heart rhythm but did not think it was anything they should worry about. Just to be sure, she suggested Tammy return for an appointment in a couple of weeks, as she wanted to keep an eye on the baby's heart. The thought of extra visits put both Tammy and Joshua's mind at ease. The doctor provided the couple with all of the necessary information for new parents and sent them to the nurses' station to schedule the next appointment. Before leaving, she told them not to worry and that all would be well. She saw this type of thing all the time and the baby was healthy without any lasting problems.

"I like her; I think I will continue seeing her as my gynecologist even after the baby is born. I'm glad she was able to squeeze us in."

"I hear she's the best and I only want the best for you and our baby . . . I thank God that all is well with the baby and he has a strong heartbeat." Joshua kissed her forehead and gave her a reassuring hug before leaving the patient room and escorting her to the nurses' station.

They were both relieved for the moment, but Tammy couldn't help but worry based on the research she'd done on Joshua's heart condition; her internet research had her all kinds of worried, seeing the worst that could happen. She knew that it was possible that the baby could have heart problems, and she wasn't prepared to deal with that. But she resolved to stand in faith with her husband, pray for her husband and baby's health, and hope that all would turn out well for their family.

# CHAPTER 35

Raegan inwardly chastised herself for keeping the knowledge of her pregnancy from Caleb, especially after the fuss she put up about him not being straightforward with her. She figured she had good reason to wait and would tell him after things settled down with Nicholas' situation. They had other things to focus on right now, and she didn't want to take the attention away from him uniting with the son he never knew he had. She gently squeezed his hand as they sat on the plane, headed to Atlanta to introduce her to Nicholas and his mother, Natalie.

Caleb rubbed her fingers.

"Are you okay? Is something bothering you?" he asked. He felt like he was more in tune with her feelings since the last heart to heart conversation they had—where they discussed Nicholas, how they would be involved, and the other things that bothered her. He felt a sense of relief when she opened up to him.

"Yes, I'm fine. You know, I'm glad that we're doing this, although I am a little nervous." She never would have guessed that she would be meeting a child of her husband's and the child's mother. She could say that this was outrageous, but not as outlandish as the situation had started when Caleb first asked her to marry him.

"Me too. Our lives are getting kind of crazy, huh?" He chuckled at the thought of everything they'd been through since they reconnected.

"Tell me about it." *And it's about to get crazier,* she added silently, thinking about the news of the baby.

Raegan tried to imagine what life would be like with their unborn child and Nicholas. How would they function? Would Nicholas come to spend a few months with them? Would her husband want to go to Atlanta and spend time there? She figured that he must not have many worries about it since he'd drifted off to sleep with his mouth slightly open. She shrugged and decided to join him before their plane landed in the next forty-five minutes.

The slight turbulence interrupted Raegan's rest each time that she made herself comfortable on her husband's shoulder. The next thing she knew, the pilot was welcoming them to Atlanta and announcing the time and temperature.

Caleb shifted in his seat at the voice of the flight attendant instructing the passengers that she was coming around one last time to pick up trash and that they should place their tray tables and seat backs into an upright position.

"Are you good?" he asked his wife after yawning and doing as the flight attendant had instructed.

"Yeah . . . and you seem to be even better considering you were snoring." She smiled and kissed him.

Raegan couldn't help but have a weird feeling about all of this. It would seem normal that a mother would want to meet the woman her child's father was with, but something didn't feel right and she couldn't quite put her finger on it.

They went through the usual procedures of picking up their luggage from baggage claim, renting a car and checking into a hotel.

Raegan had noticed that Caleb had given her a funny look earlier as he was removing their luggage from the car. Sometimes she swore that he could see right through her and wondered if he knew she was pregnant or at least had a suspicion.

"Would you like to get some rest before we meet with Natalie?" Caleb asked Raegan. He wondered if she was pregnant. Her body did look different, but he'd learned a long time ago not to ask a woman if she was pregnant. He knew most would instantly think that you were calling them overweight. Although he hoped it to be true, he decided not to mention it until she brought it up. There was no nice way to suggest to your wife that she should take a pregnancy test without any support other than "you look like you need to."

"I think I'm all right. Check to see if she's ready, and if so we can go ahead and meet with her. I can rest later."

Raegan sat on the bed and listened intently to the exchange between her husband and his child's mother, watching his body language and facial expressions. He'd never spoken much about Natalie until all of this came up, so she was very curious to know who she was and how he interacted with her.

Caleb's conversation with Natalie was brief and to the point. He exchanged a quick pleasantry with her before asking about her schedule and if they would still meet as planned. He wasn't rude but he wasn't necessarily friendly either. Part of him still harbored resentment toward her for keeping his child away from him for so long. They agreed upon a place and time to meet and Caleb ended the call.

"Are we good on the details?" Raegan asked, noticing the creases in his forehead as he put his phone back into his pocket.

"Yeah, same time and place. That means we have a few minutes," he said, kneeling in front of her and removing her shoes to give her a foot massage. Seeing how much she was enjoying it, he made himself comfortable on the floor in front of her to continue. "Cami, I appreciate you sticking with me in all of this. I know this isn't how you envisioned your life would be."

"I think it's safe to say that life has thrown us a curveball in more ways than one," she agreed, letting out a soft chuckle. "But I meant what I said at that altar a few months ago. *Forever I do.* I love you and I know that we can work through this together," she said through soft moans, enjoying the foot rub he was giving her.

When Caleb saw the kind of pleasure his wife was getting from the massage he was giving her, he couldn't help himself. He raised himself up and planted his hands on either side of her and massaged her lips with a kiss, one that he hoped proved to her in that moment how grateful he was that she was standing by his side.

∞

"Good to meet you," Raegan said, extending her hand toward Natalie after Caleb made the introductions. She smiled as she sized the woman up, surprised that Caleb had dated someone like her. She was pretty but physically quite the opposite of

Raegan. Her clothes left little to the imagination and her make-up was overdone. Raegan noticed the tattoo on her wrist as well as her different colored manicured nails and bangle jewelry on her wrist.

"Nice meeting you, Mrs. McKinney," Natalie said, accepting Raegan's handshake.

"Where is Nicholas?" Caleb asked, looking around for the little boy as they took their seats in the restaurant.

"Oh, he's not here. You'll get a chance to see him later, but we need to talk first."

"What is this about, Natalie? That was not the agreement we had," he said, looking over to his wife, who appeared to be confused as well but remained silent, watching the interaction between the two of them. She was still in disbelief that he had actually dated her.

"Chill out. He's fine but I need to talk with you about something first, so please just hear me out." She glanced from Raegan to Caleb, hoping to have their full attention.

"Okay, go ahead," he relented. He took hold of his wife's hand as they sat down, determining to listen to what Natalie had to say.

Natalie again apologized for keeping Nicholas away from him for so long and then admitted why she finally decided to show up on his doorstep. She was in no place to take care of him the way he needed, and she believed that it was best if Caleb took Nicholas for a while.

Caleb couldn't believe his ears; this was far more than he thought their meeting would be about. He felt Raegan's hand tense up inside of his. He returned the squeeze and looked at her, trying to read her expression. She looked like a deer caught in headlights. He was certain that was the last thing she was expecting to hear today. At most, they planned to meet Natalie and Nicholas, spend time with him, set up custody arrangements, and return to Houston. Natalie changed the deal and he couldn't wait to hear why.

# CHAPTER 36

*How could you give up your child?* Raegan thought. She wanted to blurt it out, but tried to be mindful not to judge Natalie. She didn't know much about Natalie, so she didn't understand her situation or know what she was going through. However, Raegan knew in her heart of hearts, no matter how tough things became, she could never willingly give up her own child. *There just has to be more to this story*, Raegan thought as she listened to her and glanced back and forth between Natalie and her husband. She could tell that he was in shock and didn't expect that Natalie wanted to place the child in his care.

"I'm sorry, I just don't understand. What is going on with you, Natalie?" Caleb asked. His mind began to consider all the possible things that she wasn't telling him. Was she on drugs? Did she no longer want to be a mother? Did she want Nicholas to stay with them forever?

"So many things," Natalie said and began to rattle them off. "Mainly severe depression. Things just aren't good for me right now and I need to go away for a while so that I can become a better mother—the type of mother he needs." Her voice was cracked and shaky. Natalie had suffered a bout of postpartum depression since giving birth to Nicholas. Because she was embarrassed to admit it or discuss her feelings with her doctor, her depression became more severe. She tried her best to explain this to Caleb and Raegan, hoping that they could care for Nicholas while she received treatment. She'd often had feelings of hurting herself and even Nicholas, and she could no longer put him in harm's way. Being in the care of his father was the best place for him right now.

"I can hardly take care of myself, so I am in no position to take care of him. I'm checking myself into a hospital and I don't know how long I'll be," Natalie concluded, her head low and eyes closed from shame.

Caleb had so many questions and this was all becoming very complicated. If he needed to care for his child, he would, but he wasn't very comfortable with the idea of Nicholas being away from his mother. What would that do to Nicholas?

"So what does this mean? What does this look like for us? Do you want Nicholas to come back to Houston with us now? What will you tell him? When will you visit him?" Caleb fired away with questions.

"Yes. He leaves with you. We can make arrangements for me to visit him when I'm ready, when I can be the mother he needs."

"Are you sure?" Raegan interrupted. In a moment of compassion, Raegan reached over and covered Natalie's hand with hers. She'd heard a lot about postpartum depression but had no idea that it could be this serious. It was hard for her to imagine what could be going on in Natalie's mind.

"Yes," Natalie muttered, bowing her head, squeezing her eyes shut. It was one of the hardest decisions that she'd made, but she was certain it was best for her baby boy. He didn't need to see his mother that way. She wanted to be a mother he could be proud of when he got older. Besides, she'd done some research on Raegan, and based on what she knew about Caleb, she was certain that Raegan would be a good influence and care for Nicholas as if he was her own.

Raegan could see that Natalie was in pain and her heart broke for her. She got up from the table to wrap her arms around the woman. She figured that whatever the woman was going through, it had to be mighty tough in order for her to even consider giving up her child. Natalie began to cry but quickly wiped her tears away with her thumbs.

"I'm fine, I'm fine. Can he come with you?" she questioned, jumping back to the matter at hand and fidgeting with her purse strap.

Raegan nodded, letting Caleb know that it was okay to give a definitive answer. There was no way she could say no to that. What kind of wife would she be? What kind of mother would she be?

"We'll take care of him. Where is he?" he asked, now a bit of excitement and anxiety creeping into his heart.

"One of my friends is keeping an eye on him for me. I'd like to spend one more night with him. I can bring him to you tomorrow with his clothes and favorite toys. Is that all right?" Natalie asked, hopeful. She tried her best to keep the knot from forming in her throat and to keep her eyes dry, but nothing worked. She'd rehearsed this a thousand times before the moment she decided to knock on Caleb's door, but that didn't make it any easier. However, she felt like this was best for Nicholas at this point in his life.

"Yes. Take all the time you need and give us a call in the morning," Caleb agreed as he stood up from the table. They had never ordered anything, but after that conversation, he didn't think he'd be able to eat for a while at this point. Natalie had given them enough to chew on.

Hand in hand, Caleb and Raegan said good-bye and walked back to their hotel, which was less than a half mile away from the restaurant where they met Natalie. The walk was silent as they pondered their private thoughts about everything that just happened.

Raegan wondered if there would be a *good* time to tell him about the baby. She figured he would probably pass out from excitement or horror in knowing that they would soon have two small children at home. She chuckled at the thought.

"Why the giggle?" Caleb asked. That was the first thing he'd said to her since they left their meeting with Natalie.

"Oh nothing. I was just thinking."

"Would you like to share? I could use a laugh right now."

Raegan smiled and switched the subject. She wanted to know how he really felt about everything. She knew that he loved

Nicholas the moment he laid eyes on him because that was the kind of man he was, but she was still concerned about the boomerang that had just been slung his way.

"I'm fine. Just surprised. A little scared. Worried. I know we were about to have a child but I'm not sure about just picking up and moving Nicholas from everything he's known the last year and taking him with us. How do you think he'll respond?" Caleb asked, stepping aside to allow Raegan to enter the revolving hotel doors first. Once he'd gone through them, he linked his fingers with hers again. "How do you feel about this?"

Raegan surprised herself. Had something like this happened a few years ago, she probably would have left him to deal with it on his own, but instead, she welcomed the idea of having a little person around. They would need the practice.

"If it's what's best for Nicholas, I'm fine with it. Every child needs a good home. My heart goes out to him and even if I did have any issues, I couldn't take them out on him. That wouldn't be fair," Raegan concluded.

Caleb thought for a moment as they went through the motions of settling back into their room. "I think she is putting Nicholas' well-being first. As his mother, if she thinks this is the right thing for him, then we are the better option. Besides, you're going to be a great mother." He smiled, pulled her close to him, and planted a kiss on the back of her neck. Raegan indeed had proved to be his favor from God; he was grateful to have her by his side.

# CHAPTER 37

"Dada Dada Dada!" Nicholas squealed as he squirmed out of his mother's arms upon noticing Caleb in the hotel lobby.

Caleb stretched his arms wide and knelt down to scoop Nicholas up into his arms, squeezing him tight. Caleb loved the feel of the boy's little hands clasped around his neck. He held the embrace just as long as Nicholas, allowing him to be the first to let go. When Nicholas finally released him, he turned to look at Raegan.

Nicholas pointed at her and smiled. He mumbled a word that sounded a lot like "pretty." He snuggled his face into his father's shoulders, pretending to be shy.

"Looks like you have another fan already. I am, of course, your biggest fan, but it looks like your fan club just got bigger." Caleb nodded toward Nicholas.

"Hi Nicholas. How are you?" Raegan cooed, stepping closer to them and complimenting him on his Elmo T-shirt.

Nicholas smiled again and buried his face in his father's neck once more. He then rose up, as if he'd found courage, and reached for her to hold him. Raegan's heart immediately melted. She had only known him a few minutes and she was already becoming attached.

"He's so sweet." Raegan smiled and played with the little boy, telling him how big and strong he looked, complimenting him on being handsome like daddy.

Natalie watched the exchange with tears in her eyes. She knew that she was making the right choice. They all seemed to fit together. She inhaled and exhaled slowly, then gathered the strength to walk over and say good-bye to her son.

"Bye-bye momma," Nicholas said, as if he understood what was about to happen. Natalie's heart broke at the sound of his words, spoken so clearly. Raegan's eyes filled with tears as well at the exchange. She knew that no matter how much Natalie thought this was best, it had to be painful.

"Momma loves you and will see you soon, okay? Be a good boy for Daddy and Ms. Raegan. Will you do that for me? You're Mommy's big boy," she encouraged, choking back tears.

"Big boy!" he echoed.

"We'll take care of him. Take care of you," Raegan whispered, hugging the woman before she left.

Caleb and Raegan stood in the hotel lobby with a car seat and suitcase filled with bottles, clothes, toys and a few diapers.

"So what do we do before our flight leaves?" Caleb asked.

"Eat?"

"Want some food? Hungry?" Raegan asked a smiling Nicholas, who was clinging to her chest, as they walked toward the hotel's restaurant to grab something to eat before leaving for the airport.

∞

Back in Houston, Caleb and Raegan busied themselves making a room comfortable and child proof for Nicholas. They were amazed at his level of energy and curiosity.

Joshua and Tammy, along with Michelle, came by for a dinner party about a week after they arrived back in town with Nicholas. They invited a few friends over to share in the new life they were starting.

"He's so handsome! He looks just like you," Michelle and Tammy said to Caleb, gushing over the little boy.

"Our baby is going to be handsome too," Joshua piped in.

"Or pretty . . . we may have a girl," Tammy said, smiling and dancing a little before returning to sit in her husband's lap.

"I am so happy for you guys. Congratulations! You're going to be a great mommy, Tammy. I'm sure of it," Raegan said, walking over to hug her friend.

As observant as Tammy was, she immediately noticed Raegan's pudge when she pulled away from the embrace. Her shirt was pulled tight around her stomach for a moment. Tammy's eyes and mouth widened in excitement, but she quickly hid her expression when Raegan gave her a warning glance. She still hadn't told Caleb yet, and she didn't want him to find out along with their friends.

Caleb was excited for Tammy and Joshua, but he knew that Raegan desired to bear a child of her own, one created by the two of them. He hoped that the news of Tammy's pregnancy didn't make her uneasy, so after Raegan hugged her, he quickly turned everyone's attention to something else.

"How about some food? I know you folks are hungry," Caleb acknowledged and everyone agreed. While Joshua and

Caleb, with Nicholas in tow, headed toward the kitchen, Raegan steered Michelle and Tammy in the direction of Nicholas' room to show off the nursery.

Raegan took her friends upstairs because she knew that Tammy was about to burst open with excitement, knowing that she and Raegan were pregnant at the same time. When they made it up the stairs into Nicholas' room, out of earshot of the guys, Tammy squeezed Raegan tight and congratulated her.

"Why haven't you told your husband, silly?" Tammy playfully tagged her on the shoulder.

"You're pregnant too?" Michelle asked, up until now fully oblivious to what just transpired.

Raegan nodded and Michelle gave her a congratulatory hug as well.

"I'm not trying to keep it a secret per se, but I wanted to find a special way to tell him. Then the whole situation with Nicholas came about . . . and we've just been on one wild ride after another. I'm going to tell him tonight. I don't think he will mind how I tell him. Poor thing will probably pass out knowing we're going to have two babies around here."

They all chuckled at the thought.

"He seems pretty content with Nicholas. I'm sure he'll be just as excited."

"Yeah . . . let's hope so," Raegan said hesitantly, ushering her friends back downstairs to join the guys for dinner.

Raegan and Caleb entertained their friends until Nicholas became irritable and was ready for bedtime. After they bid their friends goodnight, Caleb cleaned the kitchen and Raegan took charge of giving Nicholas a bath and putting him to bed. She told Caleb that she wanted to bond with him.

After bath time, Raegan put on his pajamas and read *Brown Bear, Brown Bear* to him. Nicholas enjoyed the rhymes, giggling and pointing at the colorful animals pictured in the book. When she finished the story, Raegan prayed with him and sang him a song her mother used to sing to her, even though she was off key. It didn't matter because Nicholas smiled and his eyelids were getting noticeably heavy. Not knowing that Caleb was watching them from the hallway, she told Nicholas that soon she'd be singing to him and his little brother or sister.

"We need to practice and get our stuff together so when the new baby comes in about seven months, he or she can enjoy stories and mommy's version of lullabies too," she told him, before kissing his forehead and placing him in bed. He began drifting off to sleep as soon as his head hit the pillow.

She tiptoed toward the door, making sure the baby monitor was on before leaving and quietly closed the door. She jumped when she realized Caleb was standing right outside of the bedroom door.

"Please don't do that. Why didn't you say anything?" She grabbed her chest to calm herself from the shock of seeing him standing there.

"I could ask you the same question. . . . Honey, are you pregnant?" Caleb grinned, hoping that what he'd been thinking all along was true.

She smiled and nodded.

"Yeah!" he screamed, causing Nicholas to stir in his bed.

"Shhh, you're going to wake him. I worked hard putting him to sleep," she admonished.

"I knew it!"

"What is that supposed to mean?" Raegan's eyes narrowed as she placed her hands on her hips.

"It means that your beautiful body has been ingrained in my mind; I could tell something was different," he said against her lips in between kisses. "You're so beautiful. Thank you for being everything that I want and need. And thank you for carrying our baby. I love you Mrs. McKinney."

"And I love you Mr. McKinney," Raegan said. Before she could get the words out, Caleb lifted her by the waist into his arms and kissed her passionately, allowing the kiss to indicate how happy she'd made him.

# EPILOGUE

"You have a handsome little boy," the doctor said, delivering Tammy and Joshua's eight-pound, twenty-two-inch son. They chose to wait until birth to find out the baby's gender.

Tammy was exhausted but finally relieved that God had blessed them with such a beautiful boy. The past four months were filled with countless doctor visits to monitor the baby's heart and filled with triple the amount of prayer, asking God to heal the baby before he was even born. Their prayers seem to have been answered because after monitoring the baby for twenty-four hours after birth, there was no sign of arrhythmia, the irregular heart beat the ob/gyn heard during their first visit.

His little heart was no longer skipping beats and he was breathing just fine.

"You've been worrying Mommy since the moment I knew you were there," she cooed, kissing his forehead. Joshua sat next to them on the bed, rubbing the baby's back. He continually kissed both her and the baby. He was so thankful that the baby was healthy and there were no signs of any heart condition being passed on to the baby. Joshua had fasted many weeks during Tammy's pregnancy, praying and asking God to have mercy on their baby. He didn't think he could bear knowing that the baby would have heart trouble too.

"God has been so faithful to us. I love you honey."

"We love you." Tammy kissed him and then drew both of their attention back to the baby, gently holding him up so that Joshua could look at him.

"Told you we'd have a little ball player," he said, smiling with pride.

They took selfies of them holding the baby and sent the pictures to their parents to announce the birth of Joshua, Jr. Their parents immediately called and wished them well, scheduling a time to come visit and help out for a while. After sharing the news with their parents, they called a few friends to let them know that they were all doing well.

"Caleb and Raegan are actually across the street at the doctor's office for a visit. They will stop by before heading home. Is that all right with you, or would you rather wait until you get home to have visitors? It's totally up to you. Caleb mentioned that Raegan has been extremely achy and tired lately, so I'm sure she won't take offense if you just want to rest."

"Nah, let them come on. It gives me a chance to tease Raegan about that big belly of hers one last time, especially since mine is empty now." She laughed heartily, looking at her now deflated stomach. She felt as if someone had just let the air out of her.

Joshua joined her in laughter and left to call Caleb to let him know it was fine for them to come on up.

About an hour later, Caleb entered the room along with a waddling Raegan, who was wearing a purple sundress. Caleb peeped at the baby, congratulated the couple, and took a seat near the door. He didn't want to pass any germs to the mom or new baby. He was around when his sister had children, so he remembered all of the things his mom told him about a woman's body being susceptible to germs.

"Look at you! Still waddling around. When is your due date?" Tammy teased.

"Should have been months ago if you ask me," Raegan said through heavy breaths as she took a seat next to her friend. She was breathing as if she'd just run a marathon.

The room suddenly became quiet as an exasperated Raegan said "oh no!" She realized that her water had broken as her seat became wet.

"What is it?" everyone asked simultaneously after staring at her for a few seconds. She looked as if she could go into labor at any moment.

Caleb rushed to her side and asked if she was feeling contractions. He helped her to her feet as she explained what happened. She didn't have to use many words because the water continued to seep down her leg.

"Are you all right, can you walk?" Caleb asked, with one hand in hers and the other around her waist.

"Yes . . . good thing we're already at the hospital," Raegan said with a nervous laugh.

Since they were already on the maternity floor, Caleb helped her check in. The hospital staff arrived immediately to the front desk with a wheelchair to whisk her away to the delivery room. Caleb followed closely behind as one nurse handed him a gown and cap to wear in the delivery room.

Caleb was more nervous than she was, knocking over things, stuttering and constantly questioning whether or not she was fine.

After eight hours of labor, it was finally time for Raegan to begin pushing. They were expecting a little girl and they were both excited to have both a little boy and girl at home.

At the instruction of the nurses and ob/gyn, Raegan pushed until their little girl was born, seven pounds, eighteen inches long. The nurse held the baby up so that both Raegan and Caleb could get a look at her before cleaning her up and wrapping her in a receiving blanket. Caleb couldn't have been any more in love until he was interrupted by the sound of his wife in more pain.

"What's wrong?" Caleb panicked, becoming worried that she was still in pain after the delivery.

The doctor glanced at him but remained quiet as he pressed around Raegan's belly. He looked from Raegan to Caleb and then announced that another baby was coming. Raegan's eyebrows shot up as Caleb nearly fainted.

"Another what?" Raegan asked, her heart rate elevating second by second.

"Hang on Mommy," the nurse said, instructing her to breathe and push as before.

After a few minutes, Raegan delivered a six pound, fifteen inch baby boy. After cleaning up both babies, the nurse handed one baby to each of them.

"Congratulations!" the doctor said to each of them. "I'm not sure how we missed this on the ultrasounds. I guess this little fellow was hiding."

"Once again Cami, you have over delivered . . . giving me more than my heart desires. I love you, all of you," Caleb murmured against her lips.

"I love you too," Raegan said through tears of happiness, in total disbelief, believing that God had made up for the loss she experienced the first time. She couldn't have been happier.

# About the author

In addition to reading and writing, Natasha enjoys spending her time with her husband and children. She has won the Readers' Choice award for her books, _The Life Your Spirit Craves_ and _Love, Lies & Consequences_.

Natasha believes that we were all created for purpose and inspires women to pursue their God-given purpose through her books and the _How Long Are You Going to Wait Conference_. Sign up for her monthly newsletter at www.natashafrazier.com for encouraging devotionals, current events, and new releases.

9 780098 452176